INSTEAD OF 1001 NIGHT THOUSAND AND ONE DAY

A refugee soaring to freedom

Nurgül Sönmez

FSC
www.fsc.org
MIX
Papier aus verantwortungsvollen Quellen
Paper from responsible sources
FSC® C105338

Bibliografische Information der Deutschen Nationalbibliothek: Die Deutsche Nationalbibliothek verzeichnet diese Publikation in der Deutschen Nationalbibliografie; detaillierte bibliografische Daten sind im Internet über http://dnb.dnb.de abrufbar.

Lektorat: Arzu Kaya
Korrektorat: Ömer Faruk Arslan
Weitere Mitwirkende: Gamze Taşdemir

Publisher: BoD · Books on Demand GmbH, Überseering 33, 22297 Hamburg, bod@bod.de
Print: Libri Plureos GmbH, Friedensallee 273, 22763 Hamburg

ISBN: 978-3-8482-0571-4

Imprint

INSTEAD OF 1001 NIGHT – ONE THOUSAND AND ONE DAY

Nurgül Sönmez

Translation: Nurgül Sönmez
Compilation / Editor: Arzu Kaya
Proofreading: Ömer Faruk Arslan - Berna Arslan
Book Cover Design: Gamze Taşdemir
Illustration / Index: Gamze Taşdemir

Author Contact Information:

ns.nurgulsonmez@gmail.com

nurgulsonmez

nurgulsonmezofficial

Team:

g.tsdmrr@gmail.com

nurgulsonmezofficial

nurgulsonmez

To all book lovers...

Biography

Nurgül Sönmez

21.08.1979

Germany

In the years between 1995-2020, she often received awards.

She began writing in 1995 and has written countless poems,

song lyrics and novels. Written based on true events.

The rights to over 50 novels and over 2500 song lyrics were taken over

by various publishers and famous composers.

Now she no longer stands behind the scenes,

but with her works in the middle of the stage.

Nurgül Sönmez

- Schriftstellerin -

AUTHOR'S WORKS

- Her first book ANA (Poem - Turkish) was published in **2014**
- **2015** YASEMİN'İN SAVAŞI (Turkish)
- **2017** YASEMİN'İN İNTİKAMI (Turkish)

2021

- Matilda (Turkish, German)
- 1001 GECE YERİNE - BİN BİR GÜN (Turkish)
- STATT 1001 NACHT - TAUSENDUNDEIN TAG (German)
- YASEMİN'İN ÇARESİZLİĞİ 1 (Turkish)
- YASEMİN'İN SAVAŞI 2 (Turkish)
- YASEMİN'İN İNTİKAMI 3 (Turkish)

2022

- Matilda (English)
- YASEMINS VERZWEIFELUNG 1 (German)
- MAAROUF (Turkish, German)
- INSTEAD OF 1001 NIGHT - THOUSAND AND ONE DAY (English)
- YASEMINS KAMPF 2 (German)

2023

- YASEMINS RACHE 3 (German)

2024

- YASEMIN'S DESPERATION 1 (English)
- YASEMIN'S STRUGGLE 2 (English)
- YASEMIN'S REVENGE 3 (English)
- MAAROUF (English)

All books have been translated into French and are planned for future book projects. This will be followed by translations into Arabic and Spanish. If there is interest and demand, there will also be translation in other languages.

Her works © are based on true events and she continue to support social projects with the proceeds of the books.

Soon also available as audiobooks!

Nurgül Sönmez
- Schriftstellerin -

Thousands of voices can be hope for a voice.

Instead of 1001 Nights – One Thousand One

The struggle of an eleven-years old mother with the pitched war. She disregards her life for her children while her family was killed under her eyes. The aim of her is to avenge upon murderers of her family. While she thinks she feels ready for everything, her pain is doubled with another tragic event.

Will Liya be able to withstand these difficulties any longer? Will she be able take revenge on murderes of her family? Will she be able to protect the rest of her family members, her children?

A real life story!
The traumatic story of a mother who has never lived her childhood.

Story and characters are based on real life story.

My name is Liya!

Liya means patience, **the best patience**, the most beautiful patience, **the most patient of all the patient ones.** I ask myself, after everything that has happened, do I fulfill the meaning of my name?

I was born in Aleppo on March 10, 1997. **In my childhood, I heard the birds of paradise when I flew paper birds I had made with my friends from the neighborhood.** But I only heard them when I was running to the supermarket, playing, or being chased around the corner. And suddenly, my birds of paradise were gone. The thought that they had moved away haunted me. *Would the migratory birds come back?* Would my birds of paradise return?

No. They never came back. Since that day, I have called them many times, on the street, in the neighborhoods, between the alleys, everywhere I had seen them fly before, but no sound came back. **My birds of paradise had flown away, flown away to make other children happy.** Never to return...

CHAPTER I

My father had three wives. He lived in the same house with my **mom Samira** and his **second wife Zahra**. His **third wife, Afafet, lived** in a house of her own and didn't want to live in the same house with us and be a family. My father was married to his first wife, my mother, with a civil marriage. Mother Zahra and mother Afafet were his religiously married wives. I was my mother's only child, and although I had no siblings, I had many half-siblings. **Two years after I was born, my mother Samira had to have her ovaries removed due to a serious illness.** Of course, my father didn't wait two years and married my mother Zahra. Mother Zahra gave birth to four children, three boys and one girl. After Mother Zahra gave birth to her second child, my father married Mother Afafet. His youngest wife, Mother Afafet, was sixteen years old at the time of the marriage. My father would have been about sixty-one years old at that time. Mother Afafet gave birth to five children, four girls, and one boy. **That makes a total of ten siblings with me: four boys and six girls.**

I learned to read and write in the first three years of school. After the third grade, my father, who didn't want me to go to school from the start, found excuses and stopped sending me to school. If elementary school hadn't been compulsory, I wouldn't have been able to read and write. **Although elementary school is compulsory for children up to the third grade, I was taken out of school before I had finished the three years.** Allegedly, I was kept out of school and education because

I was of marriageable age and should have concentrated more on housework and what I could learn from school. This was the first time I was deprived of my freedom.

Everyone was very careful around my father. because even with the smallest things, my father would use violence against all of us. For example, he would say, "Why didn't you put the glass of water where I wanted it?" and he would do everything from throwing the glass of water to pouring boiling water over us. He started beating us with anything he could get his hands on: with a stick, with a piece of wood, with a whip, with a belt, with a broom, with a tire, with anything you could think of. Once he had started, nobody could take anything away from him. That was my father!

I am a Muslim. We belong to the Sunni faith.

Due to our way of life in Syria, our household is very private. It is organized in such a way that no one outside the family can see the inside of the property. If necessary, an additional wall is built, but it remains closed and private. It's the same in our neighborhood. Privacy is respected. It was the same at home. At the beginning of the street, where the driveway had not yet been built, it was madc of dust and carth; it was not paved as a one-way street. But we belonged to wealthy families and knew that civil servants in our country were well off compared to other classes. **My father was also a civil servant and a registrar.** Women, on the other hand, didn't work, or rather, that was the way it was in our family. Or perhaps because I hardly ever left the house, I don't know much about life outside. So I can't say anything about it.

My mothers, Samira and Zahra, had accepted and adapted to each other. We had our own order and we continued to live without much need of the outside. We had a three-storey house. Mother Zahra and her children lived on the third floor. My mother Samira and I were on the second floor, and the kitchen, bathrooms, toilet and living room were on the first floor. From the second floor, we could go straight out into the courtyard. Most of the time we sat outside and cooked our food over the fire. **We spent our lives in the yard, far away from life outside.** We washed our dishes and laundry outside with boiling water. We made our tea outside the door and drank it together. As we lived in a hot area, we didn't know rain and only knew cold in certain winter months. That's why we always stayed outside. **We had three large covered sitting areas where we sat covered on the floor. It wasn't an ordinary seating area, however, but an upscale one.** Surrounded by tulle bows and transparent fabric bows. Seat cushions, back cushions, head cushions, and various other cushions, are all made from the same fabric.

The food was served in the center. About 30-35 adults could sit comfortably, sometimes, if we moved closer together, up to 50 adults. There was a different place for the children and the women. When we were among ourselves, we sat mixed. **It had an oriental feel.** We had a large plot of land, so to speak. It was no ordinary farm. **I spent my best years there. I spent my best years behind walls that were bigger than me.** I wish I could go back to those years.

If you love what you have,
you have everything you need..

CHAPTER 2

I was the first child to be married off. When I was eleven, I was married to a very old white-bearded man. They came from a town two or three districts away from us to ask for me. My wedding was celebrated according to the old custom, a veil was placed over my head and I was torn away from home and my family. I became the fourth wife of the white-bearded man to whom I was married. While his civilly and religiously married wives were supposed to treat me badly because they thought that everyone who came would leave, they treated me with maternal feelings because of my young age. **They soon accepted me into their midst and began to regard me as their child. I became pregnant very soon.** I was a child, but I was compelled to do so: To his wives, I was a child; to the old man I was married to, I was his wife in a religious marriage.

Anyone who sees this difference, **please do not remain silent on this issue!** Please be the voice of the silent cries. Please end this injustice, this ignorance, this child abuse, and do not turn a blind eye to this unbelievable ruthlessness. **The priority of our girls, who are just learning about life, should not be marriage but rather reading and education.** Because only with education you can have a marriage at eye level.

When I was still a child, in 2009, I had a son. His name is Ali Alhussain. **Since the woman is seen as the one who consumes and the man as the one who procreates, the birth of a boy is seen as the birth of a fertile woman.** Most of us could not accept this irrationality. Even if we thought that the woman has priority in procreation because she is the one who gives birth to children, we could not say so because we were afraid. People thought we were against men. What I couldn't understand was why only men should be glorified when it is the mother who gives birth? In this case, it should be recognized that both are necessary for the next generation.

Even before my child was born, terrible things began to happen in my country. **People took to the streets, they started attacking each other, and the sound of gunfire was getting closer by the day.** Unrest and fear filled the houses, people waited anxiously for what was to come. **The attacks that had started between the state and the people had turned into religious, linguistic, and racial discrimination.** People were killed because they were Sunni, Shia or other faiths. The call to prayer was suppressed and we were informed of the times and developments through announcements. We filled our cloth bags with as many belongings as possible and began to wait to be prepared for emergencies. **After my husband joined the crowd on the street, he never came back.** I thought *about my family every minute. Mama Samira, mother Zahra, and my siblings.*

A group of soldiers began to crowd the streets, their tanks could be seen on every corner. They began to pursue and torture everyone, guilty or innocent, as they were ordered.

They shot in broad daylight. **They didn't shoot in the air to separate people, but targeted them.** They were not separated, but collapsed where the bullet hit them. And not only that: the soldiers began to storm the houses day after day.

One of the women said: "You are the one who is closest to your father's house. We have to get youhome safely.

If your husband dies in the war, you marry his brother according to our custom. If his brother dies, you marry a relative. This cycle continues until you have freed yourself from this ignorance. **But this is not comparable to a normal marriage. It's not comparable at all. It was only for protection during the war.** As you were left a widow, the rest of the family served as your protection, and this protection was implemented in this way. There were no normal marriage relationships in it.

Assuming that the soldiers would storm our house tomorrow, they at least wanted to save me. Since we were not led by a man, who knows *what torture they would put us through.* We put on our burqas, took the cloth bags we had prepared, and set off. **We walked through the alleys, dodging here and there, but on the way, we saw that the doors of the houses and buildings were wide open.** Shots were being fired from all directions. Nobody would leave their front doors open in these neighbourhoods. This made the sight all the more frightening.

There were more warplanes and fighter jets flying overhead than I had ever seen before in my life. **I noticed that the tanks were flying flags of different colors and motifs that I knew were not from Syria.** I later learned that these soldiers waiting with their pistols, Kalashnikovs, or rifles were German and American soldiers.

What did they do in Syria? What did they want from our people? Or did our government not tell us exactly what was going on? Why were all these soldiers carrying weapons with German and American flags? When did they come, when we, as people, could not solve the problem within ourselves and realized we could barely throw ourselves into our homes, when did they come? All these thoughts and similar questions went through my mind. **When we realized that the situation in our country was more terrible than we had imagined, we moved on without lifting our heads.** After everything we had seen, I could no longer imagine anything and could only pray: "God, keep me sane."

Cars burning in the streets, stores robbed and looted, people fleeing... **People who knew they could not defend themselves left their homes.** The means of transportation were destroyed. I wanted to get to my family as quickly as possible, but we had to go as far as we had come, maybe even further.

We weren't often seen in public anyway, but the Syrian people I remembered as a whole were completely fragmented. **In addition to soldiers speaking other languages, hundreds of Syrian soldiers had declared war on our people, attacking their own country like rabid dogs**. Less than a quarter of our soldiers were trying to defend their people. Shots could be heard from all sides. We tried to approach quietly from the shore, and I had my three to four-month-old baby with me. We were constantly being stopped and questioned by soldiers. We kept walking for half a day because we were afraid they would do something to us. Eventually, we reached our father's house. I was very grateful to see him again!

Never be like those who hurt you.

CHAPTER 3

Our outside door was made of iron. No matter how hard I tried to open it from the outside, it wouldn’t open. I started banging and shouting, but no one heard me. When I realized it wouldn’t work that way, I found another entrance, and together with the woman and her two sons, we made it inside. “**Liya**”, a trembling but pleasant voice that I wanted to hear at the same time, came from the distance. I remember that from where they were, in response to the voice calling “Liya," my cry of “**Mommy**” shook the earth. **She ran towards me. I can still see it in front of me.** As much as they tried to separate us, they couldn't. We were so close that no one could separate us. They immediately took us into the house and chained the doors back on.

I had never seen our house so cold from the outside. Even the wooden shutters were closed from the outside and locked from the inside. **Without the light reflecting off the blinds, it was pitch black in the house.** I hugged my mom Samira, my mom Zahra, and my siblings as I noticed them one by one. Mother Afafet was nowhere to be seen. I asked about my father: "He left ten, fifteen days ago. He hasn't come back. We don't know," they said. As I said, life here became more difficult when there was no man. If you stayed, you didn’t know what would become of you. If you tried to emigrate, they wouldn’t let you either. **The real difficulties for women started now, we were in the middle of the war.**

Looking at our house from the outside, it looked as if it was abandoned. But the fact that everything was locked was too conspicuous. Since the door lock chain wasn't pulled out, I assumed they were home. **I wondered *if a stranger would recognize this immediately.*** Such thoughts were running through all our minds. After a brief period of excitement, we were all gripped by fear. Our connection to the outside world was completely severed, and we had no idea what was going on. **As the power was out, we couldn't follow the current situation on television.** Announcements came from the mosques. They said that civil war had broken out and that we had to leave the region for our own safety. We were informed about the situation in the region through the barely understandable loudspeaker announcements.

Every time a shot was fired, just when we thought we had gotten used to not being afraid anymore, the sound of bombs got louder and louder. The screams coming from nearby created such a terrifying atmosphere that we no longer noticed our own silence. We shook as if we were in an earthquake. We had to listen very carefully to understand what was going on out there. We had to listen very carefully to understand what was going on out there. We realized that we couldn't stay here. So we started to think about *how we could get out of here*. At home, we started talking about emigration.

My uncle lived a few houses away. That was a very rare case. The bride didn’t usually live near her relatives, but on the side where her husband lived. **The situation arose because my uncle was also a civil servant.** When my uncle was still a municipal official, my father was already retired. He was only called out in important situations. My uncle had sons who were older than us. Mama Samira jumped up from her seat and said, "Let's all try to reach your uncle. I have nephews who can protect us. Some are even soldiers. We'll take them with us and go together." She called the family together and repeated her words. My mother Zahra always asked my mom Samira about everything. Even when she wanted to do something for her children, she asked Samira for her opinion. Although she tried to get everyone's opinion when decisions needed to be made, Mama Samira had the final say in the house.

Sometimes silence is the best answer.
It can never be misquoted.

CHAPTER 4

At my mom's insistence, we gathered together and made our way to my uncle's house. We constantly checked our surroundings and each other and moved accordingly. We were careful not to make a sound, we were always on our guard.

When we arrived at my uncle's door, we saw that the whole family had gathered in the empty space around the house. We walked quickly and quietly past them. Although the outer walls of the house were twice as high as we were, we didn't have time to hug each other. The surrounding area was full of smoke and the smell of burning. The danger was not far away. It was right in front of us. As they approached, the screams rose to the sky. In panic and desperation, people tried to flee. **They were unable to react to the attacks and unfortunately, most of them did not survive.** We waited until my uncles had recovered and then decided to leave together.

We stood in the queue for migration. As I followed the queue with my baby in my arms and a diaper bag, the soldiers stopped us. **When they asked if the child belonged to me, my mom immediately said: "No, these are my two children. My daughter is carrying her brother."** When we saw the sign to move on, we kept walking and they beat those coming from behind, separated them, and took especially the boys out of the line. **The screams of the children being torn from their mothers made our hearts tremble.** Old men, young men, women, and children were mercilessly massacred.

Since we could not raise our voices even if we wanted to, we kept walking. No matter how much we thought *we could stay*, we knew we had to leave. *How many people had been injured in this endless line we were following?*

The atmosphere was never calm. **The bombs did not stop falling and the noise of the exploding guns echoed in our ears.** The increasingly louder screams were a sign that the silence could not be maintained. **The cries of the mothers filler the air dust and smoke.** I was terrified, and as my uncle and his sons looked for a place to go, they got caught up in the queue of people waiting. When they turned back, my uncle shouted, "Jordan! "We're going to Jordan. There are refugee camps there. We'll seek shelter there and come back when the war is over."

We reach the main road, the roads are now paved with asphalt. They loaded everyone into small vehicles and took them out of the city. It was the first time I had been so far away from the town where I was born and grew up. **They had taken away my home, my childhood, my life.** The streets were full of corpses. Before we left the city, they told us to wait where they had dropped us off. A truck would pick us up and take us to the Jordanian camp. **While we waited, it got dark, and in the darkness the war was even more terrible.** We imagined colorful fireworks, but the sounds were of bombs. There was another big explosion. Houses were destroyed, casualties increased, and the ground trembled.

Why did these people persecute our people? What did they have against us?

While we were waiting in fear, we saw a truck approaching. After picking us up, it drove on without stopping. Although the truck was stopped several times by soldiers, no one looked inside. **Most of the refugees didn't have any documents.** I don't even know if I had one. Every time we were stopped, we trembled with fear. We couldn't understand this persecution, we couldn't accept this torture. **We couldn't forget even for a moment that our lives were in danger.**

After a long journey, we arrived at the Jordanian refugee camp. There were more tents than I could count on a flat surface. As a family, we had to fit into the tent we were allocated. I lived there with the hope of being able to return to our homeland and prayed constantly. Life in the camp was no life at all. I wasn't expecting a particularly good situation, but we were in a situation where we had to be grateful that we were treated like third-class people. **We could only drink when the benefactors brought water, and when they brought food, we could fill our stomachs a little.** If they didn't come, we went hungry and had to drink the water from the washing-up.

We were in that camp for a long time, maybe months! **The war was endless.** *We didn't recognize hunger by the sounds coming from our stomachs,* as we thought. When a person sees their child's cries of hunger and the tears running down his cheeks, it becomes clearer that he has tasted hunger.

The camp we were in was no longer as safe as it used to be. **Soldiers were constantly coming in and out, treating us like prisoners, not refugees.** They started torturing and even killing refugees. Day by day, the refugees in the camp became fewer and fewer. Every time the soldiers came with trucks, people disappeared. **One refugee had seen that when the soldiers came, they took people away in trucks.** He advised us to be careful.

One morning, my uncle got up and said, "we can't go on like this, we can't stay here any longer. Pack your things, we're going to Idlib. From Idlib, we'll go via Bab al-Hawa. And from there, God willing, to Hatay. Our destination is Türkiye. After a few quiet nights in Idlib, we will continue on our way. Get a good night's rest and take what you need for a long journey," he said. I was shocked when my uncle told me that we had been in the Jordanian camp for a year and a half. It turned out that what I had thought was three or four months was a year and a half. How quickly the time had passed. "**Then I must be 13 years old**," I said to myself. At that moment, I realized how important it is to know the date: It was 2011.

We started with the preparations, as my uncle said, we packed our things. We met up after lunch. My uncle said, "We're leaving", at a time when everyone was still awake. That way it wouldn't look like we were running away. We couldn't leave the camp when we wanted to. We were so intimidated by the soldiers that we had to be very careful. If someone left the camp, they either didn't come back or were tortured, regardless of age or gender.

My uncle and his sons were on guard. During our stay, our valuables were confiscated. **When the soldiers began to enter our tent unannounced and brutally, the danger for us became greater and greater.** As my uncle said, we began to leave the camp in broad daylight, one by one, without attracting attention. Although they smuggled the refugees out truck by truck, the camp was full of people. *Who knows how many of our people died in the process?* When we reached our destination, we ran at my uncle's signal. We didn't look back, even if we were out of breath, we ran to survive. We had to run. Some roads were dirty, most were muddy. Although we were separated, we all got into the vehicles that would take us safely to Idlib. **We were in an endless war.** The driver warned us as soon as we got in.

"If the soldiers stop us, tell them I'm your uncle, brother, or brother-in-law, but it's better if you pretend to be asleep," told the driver.

Never ignore someone who loves you
and cares about you.
Because at some point,
this person is going to leave, and
you're never going to find someone like him again.

CHAPTER 5

We were on the street. **I was very scared.** There was smoke everywhere, bombs fell on us like rain. There were even times when it rained down on us, we were like burning coals from the smoke. When we realized it was getting closer, we ran away. **There were human bodies lying in the streets, torn apart by the explosions.** We saw human bodies, arms, legs, half heads or feet. I saw a child whose foot had been shattered, and our sons whose arms had been torn from their shoulder by the explosion. I saw mothers and fathers running away screaming with their dead babies in their arms. *What kind of massacre is this?*

Neither we nor our religion agree with such a war. The Islamic world and the religion of Islam also reject it.

I don't know how many hours we had been traveling, but the warnings and the strict control kept us silent. There were no houses or buildings nearby. Everything was destroyed everywhere, people were sad. **The streets were full of soldiers.** It was very strange, there was no call to prayer. When we saw this, we realized again the pain of losing our home. After three or four days in very difficult conditions, we arrived in Idlib. It took so long because we didn't drive at night so as not to arouse suspicion. Even when we drove during the day, the soldiers stopped us, pulled us out of the vehicle, forced us to put our hands on our heads, and interrogated us. **The soldiers who interrogated us were not our soldiers,**

even their dialog was different. They were soldiers who spoke a different language.

If they are not our soldiers, on whose orders are they in our country? Why are they waging war against our people?

I was on the verge of tears, my heart was burning in a way I can't describe. We felt the war in our souls. People were killed with bullets or tortured cruelly. I can't even talk about the mass killings.

This is not war! Our religion does not allow that. In Islam, you fight to defend your country, but you must never harm children, mothers, pregnant women, the elderly, or the sick. **You fight those who fight against you. You do not lay a hand on those who cannot fight, and you respect them.** You shall not damage a place of worship, regardless of their religion. You shall not persecute the people, or harm buildings that serve them (schools, hospitals, private service centers...). If people have to experience the war firsthand, you shall meet their needs such as shopping, food, water, and children's needs, and offer them special services. You will also not covet what the people have. Pay attention to these delicate points. This is how war is organized in Islam. I repeat: "**One may only fight in defense when one's own country is attacked.** Otherwise, a true Muslim will never wage war in this way.

What is happening in my country is an un-Islamic war. There is no such war in the Islamic world! There are soldiers from almost every country. *Who are they? What are they doing in my country? Where are our people? Why do people accept this situation instead of fighting back? Why have my people bowed down? Where are the men of my country? Why did they not resist? Why did they kneel?*

I lost my home, I was expelled from my country, and I was forcibly relocated. When I think of my house now, I bet *it's covered in dust from the bombs.* Now I am gone and will never be able to return.

Forced loneliness, abandonment.
Liya, is the living symbol of this,
that hope always exists.

She makes you rethink life with her experience.

CHAPTER 6

We arrived in the town, which belongs to a district of Idlib, in a very bad situation. We all settled into a mud house. Of course, it wasn't meant to last forever, but just to rest for a day or two and take care of our needs. We were very hungry as we hadn't eaten anything on the journey. **Water was hard to come by anyway, and when we did, we all tried to share what little we had.** The women set to work organizing things a little. The men gathered in the guest room of the house and talked amongst themselves. **When my uncle called my name in a loud voice, we all looked at each other in astonishment.** I straightened my clothes, covered my shy face, and entered. Without saying anything, I waited at the door with my head bowed. He told me that he was going to marry me off to his son because I couldn't stay alone in a war situation. I didn't have a chance to say anything, the decision had been made.

Just as I was about to turn around and leave, he called for me again. When I turned around

"I need your name for the religious wedding ceremony. Say your name. Say yes three times and please go." I did everything he said.

Liya: "My name is Liya".

Uncle: "Will you take my son Suhad-Ala as your husband?"

Liya: "Yes." (I nodded my head instead of saying yes).

Uncle: "Will you take my son Suhad-Ala as your husband?"

Liya: "Yes." (I nod my head instead of saying yes).

Uncle: “Will you take my son Suhad-Ala as your husband?”

Liya: “Yes.” (I nodded my head instead of saying yes).

I immediately went to my mom.

“Mom Samira, I have something to tell you. My uncle married me off to his son. He thought he could protect me in the war because I’m younger.”

“You got married?” she asked in surprise and smiled. She was delighted.

“We’re in the middle of a war. Your uncle has thought things through,” she said.

I got married again. I’m thirteen and it’s my second marriage. That’s how it is in war. Those who are left join forces and think that they are strong together.

The men immediately withdrew to rest. From the youngest to the oldest, they all lay down. While they lay down, the women made a fire outside and boiled water to wash the clothes. They cooked the food and washed the dishes. When they ran out of water, they boiled more water for washing. They also searched for clean water and provided it so we could wash our hands and feet. **I could give dozens more examples.**

We will be on the road without a break. And as if that wasn't enough, they say: "Aren't you finished yet? Why have you been procrastinating all morning?" I can't understand why they're like that!

No word in the world speaks louder than action.

CHAPTER 7

While we were doing the final work outside and cleaning up, a large number of soldiers attacked from the outer gate. They were desperate. They all spoke a different language. I saw the fire coming out of their eyes, they would even eat raw human flesh. We were burnt! OK, I said to myself. **It's over, we're all done for, and I wasn't wrong.** They lined us all up, brutally, pushing and shoving. They turned us around and ordered us to kneel. **We waited with our heads bowed, with soldiers shouting and swearing at us.** In the meantime, there was continuous shooting. They must have killed everyone in the house.

Suddenly, they picked out the youngest among us and dragged us into the house. Although we resisted, protested, cried, and begged, it was in vain. We were dragged into the room where the men were. We desperately begged and resisted, but it was hopeless. They killed some of us, and others were injured. **What was left of my family had to watch them rape us.** When our men, who were wounded and barely breathing, tried to fight back, they were shot either in the head or in the legs. While our screams rose to the sky, our family was forced to watch us in this state. It was an indescribable pain, I couldn't describe it even if I tried. I didn't even know how many soldiers abused us. **While each of us was being raped, my sister Rajana and I held hands and kept screaming.** They dragged us outside the house in our desperate, injured state. I heard gunshots again from inside. I think they killed the rest of us. My husband Suhad stood in front of me and saw me being raped. I was ashamed. Even if we had both survived, we could never have been spouses. Being married during the war didn't mean it was a normal marriage, it was just for protection. They had shot our mothers and brothers so that they wouldn't grow up as soldiers. Now we were in the hands of these cruel soldiers.

Rajana, mother Zahra's daughter, was eleven years old, and my other sister Ala was ten. This is child abuse, it's a crime all over the world! It must be stopped, and those responsible must be brought to justice. **This is a case that belongs before the International Criminal Court for war crimes!** We were in the hands of the soldiers, they put us in their military vehicles. They were all dirty. As three orphaned girls, we were at the mercy of unimaginable brutality. It's harsh, but they are all bastards!

We were taken to places we didn't know. We were scared and badly injured. We soon realized that they were taking us to the barracks. **There, our feet were shackled one by one with a long chain.** There were other girls and women and babies around us, just as I had my baby with me. They had rounded us up to turn us into prostitutes. A desperate criminal would pick one of us and take her. We had no one left but our master and ourselves. My sister Ala and my sister Rajana could no longer bear the cruelty and died.

I stayed there for about two years and endured their cruelty. I never rebelled, I always prayed to keep the word of God in my mouth. A soldier got me pregnant. I was ashamed, but I will have the child of rape. *That is the truth!* When I was 14, I had a son, I don't even know which soldier it was. I named him Mohamed because I thought that we needed Muhammad (peace be upon him) to end this torture. While I was crying, I said in my heart, "May our Prophet be your leader". My son Mohamed was two or three months old and my son Ali was four years old. I wanted to raise my sons bravely, God willing. When I was fourteen, I wanted to resist for my two sons as a mother.

When I was fifteen, I had another son, again by a wild soldier, I can't remember which one. I called him Omar. **My son Omar was two or three months old, Mohamed was one year old and Ali was five.** I didn't give up, we had to get out of here. If anyone made a sound, they lynched them in front of everyone or shot them without batting an eyelid. They threw the dead into a mass grave they had dug. The extent of the cruelty was unimaginable.

© Nurgül Sönmez

The Turkish soldiers came out of nowhere. They fought the oppressors and saved the oppressed. They opened fire, they took the chains off our feet. It was these glorious Turkish soldiers who saved us from these savage wolves. Our own had also fallen into the hands of these savage soldiers. The Turkish soldiers took us back to their barracks. **They saw that we had been wounded and pursued.** They took us to their hospitals where we were treated and examined. Some of us had to go to hospital. I was also taken to hospital, my injuries were very serious. They didn't separate my children from me. They were allowed to stay with me. I wanted to set foot on Turkish soil as soon as possible and kiss that soil. The Turkish army saved us all. I am grateful to all of them. They came with courage and mercy.

None of us want war. Because we have seen it, we don't want it. The people were unhappy. **I got here by walking through the migration lines that looked like a road from the air.** They were driving all these people, exploiting them, consuming them.

By what right?

They have confiscated our property, our possessions, and our bodies. Those who are waging this war, those who are on their side, cannot be human!

I had heard a lot about Türkiye and was very curious about the country and the people. I was excited as we got closer, but I was also sad to think that my country had been abandoned.

I shed more tears of relief at the war than of sadness. We were approaching the border. There were too many soldiers to cross. As I sat in the Turkish soldiers' vehicles, I suddenly saw a smile and a fiery joy filled my heart. Turkish people and Turkish soldiers were waiting for us and waved to us. **They welcomed us with open arms and kept waving to us lovingly.** What a warm-hearted people! I had heard so many good things, but I hadn't expected so much.

Before I crossed the border, I noticed an unusual commotion. Several shots were fired in succession. **People were being mutilated or shot in front of their families.** Most of the time they were killed in front of their families without looking them in the face. While fleeing from unknown soldiers in our own country, we fell into the hands of foreign-speaking soldiers. These soldiers would eat you raw, as I have described. They have no conscience, no compassion, no honor. **I am talking about soldiers who rape women in front of their husbands.** All the soldiers I saw from the age of eleven until I was fifteen were cruel. The Turkish army saved us from these soldiers who had shame written all over their faces. They fought against the traitors and tried to protect us. They opened their borders to us as if they were welcoming us with open arms. I kiss the land of such a people, I embrace it, I adopt it, I defend it, and I fight for it if I have to.

Long live the Turkish army!

Long live the Turkish nation!

Children aged ten, eleven and thirteen.
What have they left them but
their pain and their lost dreams?

Liya tries to replace the lost with her children and
welcomes mercy and patience into her heart.

CHAPTER 8

After hospitalization and treatment, I was released. The soldiers took me to the camp. It was different from the Jordanian camp. The Turkish people and the soldiers took good care of us. **We were given new clothes and we didn't lack anything.** We were surrounded by helpful people. They fulfilled our wishes and needs as best they could. *Everyone had a smile on their face, everyone smiled genuinely. They were friendly and warm. As soon as I entered Türkiye, my heart warmed and I told myself that this would be my home from now on. I embraced them, and if I had to, I would fight with this army against the oppressors. If I could be useful to Turkish society and the Turkish Republic, I would do what I had to do at that moment.* I thought and believed this way because we came out of the war.

They tried to protect us from the cruel soldiers. The glorious Turkish soldier with the Turkish flag was waiting at the border. **Just knowing that this soldier was standing there was comforting.** In this safe environment, I fell asleep for the first time. I slept very deeply. My son Omar said: "Mom, Mom, wake up! Look, the food is being distributed," he woke me up.

I got up, got dressed, and tidied up. After washing my hands and face, I went to the door. I stood in the food queue with my sons. Clean plates were being handed out. **Smoke rose from pots the size of kettles and the smell of hot food filled the room.** We couldn't believe our eyes: everyone was given their own tray, wrapped spoons, and forks, lemon-flavored wet wipes, bread, cold water in plastic bottles, lentil soup, dried beans with meat and rice. There was a small bowl of salad for the adults and pudding or waffles for the children. **I hadn't seen a meal like this for years.** The tables were arranged in rows. The four of us sat at an empty table and began to eat, giving thanks and praying. May God bless their tables too.

With each passing moment, I became more certain of my decision: **Yes, the Republic of Türkiye was to be my home from now on.** I stayed in Türkiye for two years. After years of persecution, I experienced peace here. My children could play in peace. They could be children as they wanted, without war and persecution. **That was true freedom. That was democracy.** I was seventeen years old at the time, Omar was two and a half, Mohamed was three and a half and Ali was seven.

One thing still haunted me. *What were German weapons doing in our country?* As I heard in the camp, refugees were streaming into Europe in droves. By the end of 2014, I was told that the borders had been opened. Since I can't make sense of this, I would like to ask the German government a question.

Why are your weapons in the hands of these cruel soldiers? Why were your weapons and war equipment not in the hands of those who tried to defend our country and us? You helped the oppressors, not those who defended their country. Do you think you will help us now that you have opened your borders? Did we want to leave our country? Did we want to come to your country? We never wanted to emigrate. Are you different from the oppressors who massacred my people with your weapons? You are as responsible as they are. Can you give us back our homeland now? That is impossible because you have turned our homeland into this. You have destroyed it!

European newspapers are reporting that the Turkish army has declared war on Syria. **Why are you doing this? Why are you reporting fake news and not acting courageously?** The Turkish soldiers entered the conflict to protect the true Syrian nation. You can't seriously claim that. You cannot accept that Turkish soldiers are fighting against the oppressors on the Syrian border and protecting my people.

I will ask the German and European parliaments about this. **I am determined!** Then I will turn my back on Germany and go to the Republic of Türkiye. Even if I suffer with my children on the way there, I will do it. **I have made a plan to join the queue of refugees to get to Europe and Germany.** I left the camp and followed this queue with my children. We arrived in Europe in an incredibly miserable state. We suffered a lot at the borders. Especially under the Greek soldiers. **They stripped us naked and whipped us until we were skinned.** Yes, I experienced that. Then I found a way. Although we were being persecuted, we took a ship to Italy.

On a ship at sea, without safety, with all the risks, we made our way to Europe.

When we finally arrived in Italy, Italian soldiers wanted to check our IDs. **But we didn't have any IDs.** They registered us individually and took our IDs and fingerprints. When the procedure was over, they gave each other back the documents they had taken from us. **We were still not free, because we had to stay in a camp there too.** We did what had to be done. After a few days, I found a way and a car to drive to Germany. **Yes, it was risky, but I took the risk.** I hold no grudges, I'm certainly not going to do anything bad. I just want to ask these questions and hear the answers.

"Why was my family killed by German guns?"

When we arrived in Germany, they dropped us off at the side of the road. There were other people in the car besides us. **We followed the group that got out, hid, and walked slowly towards the city center.** One of us knew the way. He led us to a refugee shelter and put us up there. I don't want to say in which city: "You stay here for one night. Tomorrow we'll go to the city council and register you," said the man who took us there. I never speak anyway, I can't even open my mouth when a stranger is around.

A day passed and in the morning the man came. We were ready and waiting. Thanks to them, they shared with us the food they had in the accommodation and had run out of.

After breakfast, we set off. It was winter and it was cold. When we arrived at the registration desk, we were asked for our details. **I would be eighteen in a month or two, so I had myself made two months older to be of age.** Then I registered my children too. We were given asylum cards. Our fingerprints were taken. They asked us where we were going to live. We were sent to another refugee home. They told us to stay there until our papers were issued. We waited more than a year and a half for these papers. I thought *Germany was a bureaucratic country.* But they did what they could. Anyway, in the end, we got our permits, even though it took a long time. **They sent us by bus to North Rhine-Westphalia to a refugee shelter.** My body was very tired. My children were no longer small. They were of school age, they had to go to school. **The German State welcomed us with open arms and was very helpful.** But I experienced racism here for the first time in my life. Of course, there were also good people, but we didn't know what to say to the bad ones. **What was racism?** *Am I allowed to be treated badly because I am Syrian? Are your standards of humanity higher than mine? How can you think that of yourselves?*

We are the same. And we will remain the same!

Sometimes it's good not to work for a short time
despite all the stress and obligations.
Because working all the time is like never working.

CHAPTER 9

The vehicles took us to the new refugee accommodation. Over 150 refugees from different countries were to be accommodated here. When we got off the buses, we were greeted by helpful people with full bags. I was nineteen years old and a mother of three children. I was so tired! **If I could just lie down once, I wouldn't wake up for months.** I was so heavy and exhausted. I was covered in dirt.

They said that we would all get a good room. We lined up and waited while they continued to distribute the bags. **While I was waiting in line, a dark-haired woman standing behind me grabbed my shoulder with one hand.** When I hesitantly turned around, she handed me the bags with a sincere smile. I lowered my head, I was embarrassed, and a sadness had settled on my face at that moment. It was as if I would cry when she touched me. She stroked my sons' heads with her loving gaze. I realized that with a wave of her hand, she wanted to say "See you inside," and nodded to her with a smile, as if to give her consent.

There were four tables next to each other at the entrance to the accommodation and we were checked by the residents. **A large police team was waiting for us. There were lots of people around the refugee center protesting against our stay.** They must have been racists, and there was another group marching against racists. As we approached, it was our turn. When it was our turn, they took our temperature and took blood and urine samples. They requested all our documents, from the ones we'd been given in Italy to the ones we'd been given at the previous refugee shelter. I collected them all and gave them to them.

Helpful people were waiting for us in the accommodation. The woman who had just come to me was looking around, I think she was looking for me. When she saw us, she came to us with an interpreter. She kissed me and hugged me with a sigh. She said in Arabic: "You have come here in pain, but you are welcome with your children". "Are you Arab?" I asked. "**No, I'm Turkish, but that doesn't matter because we're all human**," she said.

Because of this exile, no matter which country I traveled to, the face of the Turk always smiled at the oppressed.

In others, we were almost always pushed around. We never wanted that! We were driven out by force. *Is there more?* We have lost our homeland. There is no longer a country called Syria. I am devastated, I don't even have the strength to stand up anymore. **I tried to stand on my shaky legs, but after a while it was impossible.** My body was covered in wounds and I didn't feel well at all.

When the Turkish woman noticed my situation and saw my eyes watering, she came up to me with a smile and hugged me again. It was that hug. I started to cry, breaking down in her arms. She held me tighter so I didn't fall. **"An ambulance!**

Call an ambulance!" she screamed. My eyes went black. I must have fainted at that moment. I can't remember the rest until I opened my eyes in hospital.

When I woke up, I was very worried because I didn't see my children with me. Although I was on a drip, I immediately got up and started asking everyone in the hospital corridor about my children. I knew they didn't understand my language, but I called out anyway. **I was weak, my legs were still shaking.** I felt dizzy and tried to hold on to the bars in the corridor. When the Turkish woman realized that I was calling for her, she came to me immediately. She was so worried about my condition that she hurried. I immediately asked about my children: "Don't worry. They are in good hands," she said. She tried to allay my fears with her words. **I thought she was a trustworthy person and believed her.** She took me by the arm and led me to my room. She may not know what I was going through, but she seemed to sense it.

She had called a close friend to interpret so that we could understand each other better. She tried to tell us that she would be coming soon and that we would then be able to understand each other better. Someone from social services would be coming tomorrow. **I told her my name was Liya and she told me her name was Nurgül.** I looked exhausted. I was very sad. I looked forty, even though I was not yet twenty. My head was slightly down, I was ashamed and angry about my situation. We were defenceless and I had suffered a lot at the hands of the oppressors. I had lost my whole family, even my brothers and sisters had been separated from me in the Jordanian camp. I looked for them, but I couldn't find them. ***They were probably among the refugees who were taken away in trucks.*** I cried the whole time, my heart was still burning and aching. *I had experienced atrocities and seen dead people. I was raped as a child, defenceless, in front of my family. For two years I was abused as a prostitute by cruel soldiers, my feet were in chains. I was devastated.*

While I waited for the interpreter and the people from social services, these thoughts ran through my head and tears welled up in my eyes. *How can I describe this pain, how can I make up for it?*

I have to keep my wits about me, God! The Turkish woman tried to comfort me during this time. She couldn't even imagine what I was going through. We heard the door click and the people we had been waiting for were there.

"Liya asked what had happened and why she was in the hospital, and her interpreter tried to comfort her with a hug. **When she started talking about her experiences, we realized that Liya was suffering from psychological trauma.** Inpatient treatment would do her a lot of good. From what she showed, her body had suffered many injuries. But the treatment she truly needed was for the wounds to her soul. Her whole body bore the scars of persecution."

I knelt on my knees and sobbed and cried as I recounted one experience after another in that hospital room. My pain was unbearable. **Believing I was in good hands, I had let myself fall like this.** For the first time, I was so relaxed that I felt safe. I broke the shackles I was holding on to, so much so that I passed out again while I was telling the story.

When I came to, the Turkish woman was holding my hand. I started coughing and they put me on the bed. The interpreter was sitting in the chair opposite, the other woman was nowhere to be seen. The interpreter worked as an administrative employee in the city administration. While I was unconscious, the doctor came into my room and the interpreter told him everything I had told her. They said I needed inpatient psychological treatment. **They told me that my children were in good hands and that I would get them back when I was released.** I believed and trusted them and agreed to inpatient treatment.

The hospital for nervous and mental illnesses was contacted. I was told that I would be transferred there a day later. **They took me to see my children for the last time.** I knew that I really needed this treatment. As a mother, of course, I should have been with my children, but what I went through was very difficult for me as a child. The better and stronger I was, the better I could raise my children, but if I continued to have health problems and wasn't strong, I could never guarantee that my children were safe.

After several other doctors had treated me, I finished the examinations and was taken away by the psychologists. My interpreter and the Turkish woman Nurgül never left my side. They accompanied me until I was discharged and helped and supported me with all the necessary steps.

There are two ways to be wrong:

one is to believe it is not true.

The other is not to believe what is true.

CHAPTER 10

I was taken to the psychiatric hospital by ambulance. The journey took about two hours. As I lay on the stretcher, I slept without interruption. I realized how tired my body was. **I was so tired that I desperately needed to rest.**

We arrived and they gave me the reports. I didn't have the Turkish lady or my interpreter with me. Not to mention the lady from social services who came, wrote, signed, and left again. She was very important. It wouldn't have been possible without her. But since we changed cities, she is no longer the official who looks after me. I only found out the other day before I was sent away. My registration took a long time. **When I realized I couldn't walk on my own, I met a nurse who indicated with a mocking smile that she wouldn't take my arm.** There was a wheelchair. I pointed to it with my hand to ask if it was okay. She said something like, "Go get it yourself," in an angry manner as she continued to grimace. **As a sick and injured person, I needed respect and love above all else.** As the doctors called me to a different room for each examination, I had to put myself in the hands of the nurses. How were they supposed to treat me without an interpreter? *How could I explain my problems, worries and experiences?* I asked for an interpreter. I thought that *if I said interpreter, they would understand me.* I had great difficulties. After all the treatment and admission procedures, I was admitted to a closed ward. I was alone in the room, no one came or went.

I had no luggage. I only had a change of clothes that I had been given in the refugee accommodation. **A nurse came into my room and told me that I had to take medication.** She told me to take it in front of her. After I had taken it, she looked closely into my mouth to see if I had truly swallowed it. *Why shouldn't I swallow it,* I thought, and then I got tired and fell asleep. I couldn't tell her about my problems, so I thought *it was just another problem.*

Some of the nurses were very nice, very friendly and helpful. When they came into my room, they tried to explain everything to me with their hands and body movements so that I could understand. **But there were also situations where I didn't want to put myself in their hands.**

That day, I silently did what they told me. It was dark. I couldn't speak a single sentence, I couldn't say anything, nobody came or went.

Only those who are not satisfied with themselves mistreat others. Remember that.

CHAPTER 11

Three weeks had passed.

The floor I was on was closed to visitors. I knew nothing about it since it was closed. **The interpreter came and went three times in three weeks, to be precise.** Thanks to her, I was able to communicate with the doctors and therapists, she understood me well and stood up for my rights. That gave me strength. She contacted social services in my town to provide me with an interpreter once a week. If necessary, she agreed to two interpreters. **As I was on the closed floor, Nurgül, the Turkish woman I had met, couldn't visit me.** I found out that only the staff had access and immediately asked about my children before I asked about myself.

"Don't worry. We didn't hand your children over to an orphanage. I have tried very hard. I told them that the children couldn't be taken anywhere else but to Family and Social Services. Everyone in that place stood up with me. They said in a loud voice that we were their parents. They can't take them anywhere, they said. **Many humanitarians risked their lives so that the children could grow up with us.**

I had to leave immediately because I didn't want my children to be taken away from me. I told everyone who came in that I had to be with my children. I didn't feel comfortable. **Thanks to the interpreter, she secretly connected me to my children via video call every time she came in.**

I cried, but with joy. The more I saw that they were doing well, the better I felt.

The interpreter's name was Jamelia. She was very demanding every time she came. She asked and found out everything, from the pills I was given to how long I would have to stay here. Each time she was told that, as a war victim, I had to receive more important treatment and that I couldn't leave the closed ward for a certain period of time.

"But she doesn't even speak your language, she can't talk to you, they keep giving her medication and putting her to sleep," Jamelia said to the doctor.

She defended me. In the first few days, it was good to rest and sleep, but this couldn't go on. My family had been killed and my heart ached. I wouldn't even be able to attend their funerals and visit their graves. I didn't even know if they were buried somewhere or placed in the mass graves. I had been expelled from my homeland. *What could be worse than that? Now I thought that if they tried to take my children away from me, they would see Liya turn from a lamb into a wild wolf. If that was their intention, then I could be a wolf, I had already suffered so much, what else did I have to lose?*

There wasn't even a TV in my room, I wanted to watch the news. I had a bed, a chair, and a wash basin. That was all. When Jamelia mentioned that,"She could injure or even kill herself. That's why we have to take precautions," they said.

Which suicide? Who kills himself? God is the giver of this life! No one can take it but Him! If I had tried to kill myself, I would have killed myself when I was in chains, I would have killed myself when the war started, I would have killed myself when I was raped in front of my family by an unknown number of soldiers, I would have killed myself when I was in exile, in a Jordanian refugee camp, or when I tried, under whatever difficulties, to get to Europe. How old am I? I didn't kill myself when I experienced all this cruelty and torture, and I wanted to kill myself in this room in front of them. What a logic! God gave me this life and only He can take it away from me. **No matter what faith, God is one!** I respect all faiths, even non-believers. **Everyone is allowed to live the way they want.** No one is allowed to judge anyone for that. No one can judge me because my faith is Islam and I am Syrian. What rights do they have? No more than I have the right to condemn anyone.

There have been nurses who have hurt and harmed patients through their behavior. Imagine a box of tomatoes, not all of them are rotten, but there can be healthy ones too. Just like these nurses in the healthcare system. I had gradually eliminated the unscrupulous and ruthless ones, I just didn’t understand their language, and because I didn’t understand them, some reacted by shouting. **I just didn’t understand their language, why did they have to shout?** I wasn’t deaf!

I signaled with my hands that I didn't understand what they were saying and there was no point in them getting angry and repeating it. I heard well enough, but I didn't understand anything, but they kept shouting anyway instead of finding a solution. But I wasn't deaf, I heard well.

Although Jamelia had asked for an interpreter for me days ago, there still wasn't one. There was a volunteer interpreter who came to the people who needed him two or three times a week. But because I was isolated, he wasn't allowed to come to my floor. He had to be a sworn interpreter. I wasn't the one who embarrassed the state. I could have spoken to the volunteer interpreter and told him what was needed. I was no longer incarcerated here, and the thought of *taking the place of someone else who really needed it* tormented me. **I insisted on being released.** In the first few days, I was very tired and needed rest and sleep. But even after those days, I still didn't understand why I was isolated and behind closed doors. *What was the point of staying there if I wasn't understood?*

Shortly afterward, another tragedy occurred when a nurse wanted to change the bed linen. She asked me to get out of bed. *How was I to know that she was talking to me outside the door without looking me in the face?* Because she was standing in front of the door, I thought she was talking to another nurse. Even if she had said it to my face, I wouldn't have understood what she was saying! I understood a few words, it always depended on how you pronounced them. I was not yet able to form sentences.

How could I? I hadn't done a language course yet because I was still waiting for my papers. When I finally got them, less than three days later we were taken to other accommodation in several buses. It should have started in my new accommodation. **I don't know their language yet and I can't speak it either.** I don't understand why this is not tolerated in this country. **Then she closed the door from the inside with a jerk, grabbed me by the nightgown, and threw me off the bed onto the floor, angry and frustrated. She lunged at me like a fury, tore at my headgear with all her might, grabbed my hair with her hands, rolled it in her fists, and smashed my head on the floor several times with all her fury. She started screaming for help as I reacted to what she was doing and why she was doing it. After pushing a button in the room, she kicked me in the ankle, causing me to fall to my knees. She threw me to the floor and laid me on my stomach and pushed on my back with one hand and her knee. I don't know how many nurses and guards stormed into the room as a result. Her anger and rage had not abated, and she squeezed my hand with her knee.** Then she said something and handed me over to the guards. They beat me in the closed room until I was completely blue. I didn't even realize what was happening. I didn't even know why the bodyguards were beating me.

They tied me to my sickbed, battered and bruised.

First, my hands were tied one by one, then my feet were tied to the edge of the bed. As if that wasn't enough, they also tied a strap around my shoulders and knees. *I wasn't an attacker, what state have you put me in?*

I was brought here because I was wounded, I am lying here so that you can give me medicine, not so that I can be wounded even more! You gave me an injection to make me sleep. I don't know when I woke up, but when I woke up I had severe pain all over my body. **My eyes were swollen so that I couldn't see, not because I could see that they were swollen, but because I could feel it because my eyes wouldn't open.** Although I couldn't touch my hands, I could feel that my lips were swollen and burst open. **With my hands tied, I cried on my bed.** *Why was man persecuting man, killing man, torturing man? Which of them should I pity? What should I close my eyes to? What torture and cruelty can I still close my eyes to?*

I couldn't even wipe my tears because my hands were tied. *What kind of humanity was that?* **This was injustice and a crime!** I swore to myself that I wouldn't accept it. Imagine there was a war in my country and I was being cruelly tortured. I realized that there is no justice in war. There is true justice in war. There are rules and laws. *But what if you're in the middle of Europe and you're being tortured?* **I stayed in this hospital, where I was admitted as a wounded person, to get better, not to get more wounds!**

The nurse who dehumanized and tortured me continued to bring me my medication and forced me to drink it. Since my upper lip was swollen, I couldn't feel the glass she held to my mouth touch my lip. I was still preoccupied with my bound state. **Then she looked at my face, smiled mischievously and poured all the water from the glass over my face. After making sure I had swallowed the pill from my mouth, she spat in my mouth in addition and left.** Every time she entered my room, she would start abusing me, hitting me, pinching me with the door open, or angrily explaining something to me. I even had traces of her fingernails on my cheeks. I remember her putting my pills in my mouth and pressing her fingernails into my flesh as if to examine it. **My face was covered in bruises, even though I hadn't caused any trouble.** *How could I cause trouble when I was tied up?* I hadn't been brought in as an aggressive patient, I was wounded, tired, a victim of war.

This woman should never be a nurse! She lacks humanity. She should never have been allowed near patients. **Such people should be brought to justice and receive the harshest punishment.** If you cause more harm to an injured patient, you can't call that health or justice! This is a crime and the crime must be punished!

Fate is that two people who have
never called each other find each other.

CHAPTER 12

One day, Nurgül surprised me in my room and came with a nurse, a woman I had never seen before and who seemed nice to me. **As soon as Nurgül saw me, she put her hand over her mouth and looked at me.** She seemed to be in shock. Then she came closer and closer to my bed, to which I was tied. When I saw her like that, I felt sorry for myself for the first time and started to cry. I thought *someone was coming to me who understood me.* She must have noticed and seen that something was wrong. It wasn't as if you couldn't see it!

I hadn't seen myself in this state yet, but I only felt my condition through my pain. Then she allowed the other lady, who was still a stranger to me, come closer. Then Nurgül withdrew and leaned against the wall, terrified. **The nurse first bandaged my open wounds with what she had with her.** In the meantime, she realized that I didn't speak German and tried to explain herself with gestures so that I understood her. We got to know each other by saying our names: I am Liya and I am Palmira. **She would have liked to untie my hands and feet, but then she would have been in big trouble with the court.** She stroked my hair and wiped away my tears. Sister Palmira gave me a sign to collect myself for a moment and quietly left my room with a tearful smile on her face. Nurgül followed her.

When she came back, she had a cell phone in her hand and took photos of all my wounds where I had experienced violence. She left quietly, again with a sad smile. **A short time later she came back, but this time not alone. She had a file under her arm and a nurse who spoke Arabic.** The lady I had thought was an optimistic nurse turned out to be a senior doctor. I should have called her Dr. Palmira from now on, as was proper. She didn't come into my room empty-handed but with a tape cassette. **The nurse's assistant, the senior doctor's assistant so to speak, was supposed to act as an interpreter and record what I said.** First I met the assistant, she said her name was Dia. The doctor turned out to be Turkish. Again, a Turk smiled at me and helped me. The saying "The Turk is on the side of the oppressed" is burned into my brain.

There was only one chair in my room, which the senior doctor pulled up to my bed. "Would you like to sit down?" she asked **Nurse Dia.** When she replied, "No, please sit down," Dr. Palmira sat down next to my bed. First I was asked if I agreed to my voice being recorded on tape as evidence. Of course, I agreed! **However, I realized that I was having difficulty speaking at all because of the injuries I had sustained.** My lips were swollen, but I could understand what I was saying. We tried a few sounds and the senior doctor, Doctor Palmira, asked me point blank: **"Are you ready?"** Yes, I was ready.

"After I turn on the tape, I'll put it on you, and then I'll give you the necessary information about the contents of the file and ask you questions," she said.

She asked me to concentrate.

"**What happened to you is a criminal offense. I will try to clear up the matter with the evidence available to us,**" she said.

I trusted her. Unfortunately, she said she would have to keep me tied up until we had a legal result. But she promised it wouldn't take long.

"Dia will translate everything I say into your language. She will translate everything you say into German for me." "**Here we go,**" she says, continuing to stroke my hair.

Dr. Palmira: "I am a senior physician in the Department of Neurology and Psychiatry, my name is Palmira. I am in room 102 of the closed psychiatric ward, the room of Liya, who suffered serious violence and physical injuries at the hands of the staff and employees of our hospital. I found her face swollen and bruised, her hands and feet tied to the bed, and as if that wasn't enough, they had also put straps around her shoulders and knees. As victims of war, we agreed that our patient Liya could recover in our hospital for a few more days. In order to obtain more detailed information, my medical colleagues and I decided together that she should stay in our hospital.

(She talked about file information, a brief summary of war events, etc.).

The assistant Dia, who is currently in the room, speaks the same language as our patient Liya. She will therefore act as an interpreter to pass on the information to the patient. She also explains that she will witness this recording.

A friend who doesn't work in our hospital contacted me on my private phone. She really wanted to visit Liya, but as it was a closed ward, she couldn't. I asked her to come to me so that we could visit her together. After she arrived, we wanted to make an unannounced visit together to Liya, a patient who had just been admitted a few months earlier.

When I got to her room and found her in a very bad state, I had to intervene. As we didn't speak the same language, my first thought was to ask my assistant Dia to help me as an interpreter. As soon as I left the room, I called her and asked her to visit me in her free time. Fortunately, she was very helpful and came immediately. **I consider what I heard to be inhumane and demand an immediate investigation.**

I give the floor to Liya, who answers my questions while our interpreter translates, as can be heard on the tape.

Liya: "It's a bit difficult for me to speak, and I want to emphasize that right at the beginning. When I first arrived at the refugee center, I was admitted to this hospital to receive psychological treatment. After the initial examinations, I was referred to the hospital. I thought that I would *find ointment for my wounds in this hospital,* but I experienced the opposite. I was admitted to the closed ward. Although I was told it would only take a day or two, I was kept here for weeks. The interpreter I had met in the refugee center always came to help me. But now she doesn't come anymore. I don't know if she won't be let in because I'm on the closed floor.

I don't speak German, not at all in fact. I've only learned a few words since the day I arrived. I've never been to a language course. Or rather, I don't know if I had the right to. I have three young sons. They are still in the refugee home. I would like to learn German, but I know it's a matter of time. That's why we need the assistant Dia at the moment. I am very grateful to her.

When I arrived, I slept most of the time because I was very tired and had been given medication. After I rested and got enough sleep, I felt energized and thought *they could get me out of that room.* I felt rested and ready for the therapy sessions. I told this to my interpreter at the time and she passed on what I had said to anyone interested. Then I realized that the medication was making me sleepy and weak, so I felt weak and powerless. Without objecting, I said in an appropriate language, "I don't want to take this medication, it's too heavy for me," and Jamelia finally said, "The medication is obviously too heavy. Can you reduce the dose?" Jamelia asked. When she saw that there was no change in my condition, she knew that her request had not been heard.

Jamelia, who had applied for an interpreter for me, told me that she had filled out the application. At the time, volunteer interpreters wanted to help, but as the floor was closed, only a sworn interpreter was allowed in. . *If I couldn't talk about my injuries here, what was the point of staying here or being admitted as an inpatient? Was I here to aggravate my injuries?* In that case, there would have been no need to intervene, I would have stayed with my sons. I ask about my sons, with whom I can no longer even communicate:

Where are they? What are they doing right now?

Since the day I was admitted, a nurse who works on this floor has been swearing at me. **I don't understand what she's saying and she starts shouting at me. But I'm not deaf! We just don't speak the same language.** Day by day, her behavior in front of the others got better, and day by day, her behavior between the two of us got uglier.

What the hospital staff did was unimaginable! The catering staff left after leaving my food in my room. During meals, my left hand and leg were untied by a male nurse. The food was handed to me so that I could sit down, on the condition that my right hand and leg remained tied. After the orderly had done this and left my room, the person who had handed out the food came back into my room. At breakfast, he took the bread from my plate and left me slices of salami. He was similarly unfriendly at lunch. Jamelia had dictated that, as a Muslim, I was not allowed to eat everything, and my food was distributed accordingly. After I had eaten lunch, the orderly checked my food, untied me, and left the room. Everything happened after he left. Secretly, the caterer came with another tray and changed my food. Instead of vegetarian dishes, I found a menu with pork on my plate. I either dipped my fork in mashed potatoes without gravy or tried to fill up on the fruit, salad, and cakes that were served on the side. It was better than nothing, I didn't complain. I was often hungry, but I thought that there *had to be a reward for this, that a miracle would happen soon.* Dinner was normal as it was distributed by another member of staff. The morning and lunchtime staff only did this when I was restrained. So did the nurse who was working at the time. I had the feeling that they were checking up on each other about me. I also noticed that they knew each other when they talked from time to time..

Because of our language difference, many nurses in the hospital have shouted at me. I can recognize them all and point at them when I see them. Another incident:

The nurse grabbed me by the collar and pulled me out of bed. She pushed me, grabbed me by the hair, and banged my head against the walls, the floor and the metal bed frame. I was slapped countless ttimes, but the last time was the last. *I should have intervened the first time,* but as I didn't speak her language, I couldn't complain.

She set me up and abused her position. After she called security and said something I don't know what it was, she had me beaten up. Since that day I've been confined to bed. I'm all blue and in pain. I complain about that nurse. I don't know her name, but I recognize her when I see her. Apart from her, two or three other nurses treat me like this. They shout at me all the time, look down on me, and belittle me because I don't speak their language. During the obligatory administration of medication, they dug their fingernails into my cheeks.

The marks are still visible on my cheek and will probably remain a memory. I am constantly tortured, they twist my fingers, pinch me, bite my flesh, push me. They all have the look of a bully on their faces.

As I lay tied up on my bed, Dr. Palmira entered my room unexpectedly. From the look on her face, I understood better that my condition did not seem normal. It was obvious that she had not expected such a sight when she saw the patient. She covered her mouth with her hand and came to my bedside. Dr. Palmira was the first person in this hospital to treat me like a human being. Now she is trying to defend me by taking my tape recording and risking her own job. I would like to thank Mrs. Palmira from the bottom of my heart, that's all I have to say at the moment".

Dr. Palmira: "For the time being, I am submitting this audio recording and the photos I took to the court as evidence".

I cried, and Dr. Palmira tried to comfort me by stroking my hair. She was so young that I thought she was a nurse when I first saw her.

"Let's not waste any more time. I can't bear to see you tied up like this any longer. Sister Dia will stay with you until I return. Are you ready for this slow journey now, Liya?" she asked.

I replied: "Doctor, I've been through so many phases, I'm more than ready for this". The doctor left the room with the tape and the file.

Half an hour later, she came back. This time she had the police with her. She played them the tape and let them listen. Other doctors wanted to enter the room. Among them there were doctors who had done violence to me, who ignored this condition and acted against it. I told this to the nurse Dia, who translated it into German and informed the police. I was asked to show them which doctors they were. I did and their statements were to be taken.

Police: "Well, did you see these violent people today or did one of them come into your room?

Do you know their names? Would you recognize them if you saw them?"

Liya: "Yes, I saw one of them today, they entered my room and tortured me again and treated me inhumanely. I would recognize them all if I saw them, and I would also recognize the guards who came into my room and did this violence to me. I was not admitted here as an aggressive patient but as a wounded and injured victim of war. Instead of being treated with compassion and love, they added countless more wounds to my many wounds."

I cried again.

The doctor's assistant entered the room with a piece of paper in her hand. After giving the note to Mrs. Palmira, she said,

"Good news, we can untie your hands and arms with a court order."

As she untied me , the doctor's eyes began to water. She must have been touched by my situation too because she couldn't hold back her tears. She secretly tried to wipe her tears away so as not to show her emotion. I was finally untied.

The police officers asked: "Do you have a photo of the staff on this floor?" They said there were photos of all the staff. "Well, is it in the file who is taking care of patient Liya?" they asked, and the answer was that it wasn't in the file, but on a sign in the nurses' room. This sign was checked. "I want copies of all these signs from the day Liya was admitted until today," the police officers said. There was a flurry of activity among the nurses. The door to my room was open, I could see people walking past and, of course, as it was a closed floor, no visitors were walking through the corridors. *If even the patients weren't allowed to leave their rooms, who else could walk around apart from the officers and staff?*

When the room was quiet again, Dr. Palmira told me that she had a nice surprise for me. She said that **she would take me from the closed floor to the room next to her office on the second floor and that from now on Nurse Dia would be my personal nurse who would take care of me**. I was happy to hear this news. She advised me that it would be better to stay here until my serious injuries from the violence had healed.

Although she told me not to worry, and that we had many volunteer interpreters, I didn't worry about anything except ***my children***. My thoughts only revolved around them.

There was no word from those who had taken me in about Jamelia and the lady from social services, whose name I didn't know. I was very upset and spoke to Dr. Palmira about it before I changed rooms. I wanted to talk to Jamelia while the police officers continued their search on the closed floor.

When I told Mrs. Palmira, "Jamelia's cell phone number is on a slip of paper in the pocket of my everyday clothes," she called the nurses and asked them to bring me my clothes. My clothes were brought, but as my everyday clothes had been washed, the phone number on the note was no longer legible. When I asked, "Why did you wash them?", they mumbled amongst themselves, "They must be full of germs, that's why they washed them". Sister Dia immediately translated the conversation into German for Dr. Palmira. I thought that *good would prevail.* Of course, the senior doctor intervened immediately, reacted terribly and intervened.

Dr. Palmira was surrounded by many helpful people. She gave instructions to each of them and they all followed them. **She was a very influential senior doctor.** Unexpectedly, the head doctor arrived. While all the doctors were standing, he approached Mrs. Palmira.

Chief physician: "What's going on, doctor? Is what I'm hearing true? We have to find out who did this immediately. I can't let them stay in our hospital one second longer."

They retired to their rooms.

Of course, I only found out about these conversations later, although I didn't understand what they were muttering.

One of the most important things to learn to master life is to stay "calm."

CHAPTER 13

She started preparing to take me to the second floor. To get from my room to the elevator, we had to walk through the hallway. I had become so anxious by then that if someone walked past me or suddenly approached me from behind, I would flinch and become very frightened. Of course, I wanted to get over that. *Who knows what that nurse told me that made the guards, nurses, and carers react like that.* I wasn't aggressive! If the nurse wanted to change the bed linen, she could have come into my room in a friendly manner, shown me the comforter with her hand, and made it clear with a gesture that she wanted to change it. If I hadn't gotten up immediately, I would have even offered to take the blanket from her hand and change it myself so as not to burden her. As she shouted louder and louder at me, I said in my mother tongue: "I'm not deaf, please don't shout! Just because we don't speak the same language doesn't mean you have to shout", whereupon she attacked me with kicks and slaps. Then it happened as it had to. The room was full of bodyguards and nurses. Just because we don't speak the same language doesn't mean I'm deaf!

What kind of view, what kind of thought is that?

On the way to my new room, I said to Sister Dia: "I'll pass all this on exactly as it is. It's good that you said that in the voice recordings. But you should stay with me for now. I hope we'll take care of it," she said. I found it hard to stand and walk because they beat me all over my body with their fists and, when they got tired, they continued to beat me with a truncheon. **Sister Dia put me in a wheelchair.** The doors to the second floor were open and there were no two armed guards in front of them. The patients could walk through the corridors without any problems. I no longer had to enter a password at the entrance to my room. You could enter as soon as you opened the door. **The beds were different, the contents of the room were different, the windows could be opened, and you could watch TV, it was completely different from the closed ward. There was a desk, a wardrobe, and two chairs. So it was a hospital room as we know it.** But it was clear that the people who came here had furnished the room very nicely and spaciously because they stayed for a long time.

There was still something I didn't understand. ***How could they put me in such a closed room without listening to me, without talking to me? Am I a child molester? A terrorist? A serial killer?***

No, no, no, no...

For those who commit these atrocities, such a place is appropriate.

I am a victim of the war. I just wanted to come to terms with what I had experienced. I didn't want to wake up at night with nightmares, startled by the deafening noise of bombs and gunfire. I also didn't want to be attacked by soldiers while being chased by soldiers. I just wanted to get rid of my nightmares. I didn't want to have any new nightmares.

There was a full-length mirror in the room. I was wearing a special nightgown that belonged to the hospital. **I stood in front of the mirror and looked at the wounds on my body.** Even I couldn't imagine how bad they were. I had blue, purple, green, and other colored marks all over me. From my legs to my arms, from my thighs to my back. My face was swollen and blue, with open wounds that had burst open. My face was completely disfigured and my head hurt. When I ran my hand over my head, I also felt the crusted wounds. I couldn't imagine that I was in such a terrible state because I hadn't seen it on the second floor. I couldn't even guess. While I was still looking at myself in the mirror, a very nice and friendly nurse came into my room. And next to her, of course, was Nurse Dia.

Nurse Jenny: "Hello Liya. I'm Nurse Jenny. Welcome to your new room. Dr. Palmira sent me. **I'm so sorry, whoever did this to you must have been a savage beast.** I want them punished as soon as possible. If you don't mind, I can take a look at your wounds, they are horrible, horrible, horrible....

I don't know what to say. You are about to undergo a series of examinations. Please prepare yourself now. **We need a report on every inch of your body.** I am here to take care of your immediate needs. I also want to discuss with you the daily routine and the rules of the duty days. That's not difficult. Would you like a cup of coffee or tea while we talk?"

Liya: "Hello Sister Jenny. I'm very happy, you're very friendly. Believe me, your kindness is very good for me at the moment. If I was wrong, I can understand that, but I wasn't wrong, so I want them to be punished. **All I need are my children.** I don't want anything else, food or drink if I have to. Just bring me my children. Thank you, of course, I stick to the rules and the daily routine. I will never break the rules. I'll do everything you say. Thank you, Sister Jenny.

Then Nurse Jenny brought me some clothes to wear. They were probably old clothes from patients at the hospital. I had to take them because I needed them. There was a shower cubicle in my room. It only belonged to the patient in the room. I couldn't move one arm at all and it hurt a lot. She helped me shower and put on the clothes she had brought. Nurse Jenny's smile was not fake. You could tell she was an optimistic person. **She was comforting. After all the inhumane treatment and evil I had seen, this was the smile that would heal my wounds.** She combed and braided my hair lovingly.

When I started talking about the rules and the daily routine, another nurse came into the room. She took me for a CT scan, an MRI scan and an X-ray. Together with two female doctors, every inch of my body was photographed. I was badly injured. After all the examinations, nobody treated me badly. Everyone was very nice to me and everyone treated me with guilt. But only criminals should feel guilty. There was no reason for them to. I felt that with all the doctors and nurses.

It wasn't long before Sister Jenny came into my room with a tray of hot coffee, two slices of cake, and a banana. At first, I ate as if I hadn't seen what she had brought me. I was very hungry and as they kept taking my food away, I was starved down to 39 kg. **This cruelty was inhumane, and Sister Jenny was aware of it. She, who had done nothing wrong, could not hold back her tears of guilt.** That was what it meant to be human. She was very calm and patient and did not leave my side until my meal was over. Sister Dia became my tongue, my mouthpiece. My body was exhausted after eating so much and I was helped to lie down on the bed. In bed, I fell asleep immediately.

Dr. Palmira didn't come into my room for a long time. When I woke up, Sister Dia had asked her mother for food and had it brought to the hospital. I couldn't believe my eyes, I was so hungry, it was unimaginable. **She had thought of everything, from the soup to the main course to the dessert.** When Sister Jenny saw this, she left the room and tried to hide her tears from me. I felt sorry for her, what a strange situation.

I was so tired that after washing my face and hands again in the evening, I slept until the morning. I couldn't sleep on the second floor because I was scared. I didn't have a proper sleep rhythm. When they came into my room at night, I was afraid that they would torture me. That night, for the first time, I was able to close my eyes and sleep peacefully despite my pain.

When I woke up in the morning, Dr. Palmira was standing in my room. She smiled at me and said: "Good morning". As I had learned this word in the refugee home, I said "Guten Morgen" to her in German. She gave me a sign that she was coming and left the room. When she came back, she brought a young woman with her to translate. She was also a nurse. "In a democracy, resources are not exhausted". "We don't necessarily need a sworn interpreter to get along. **You can also communicate with body language if you have to.** As long as it's people," said the young senior doctor, Mrs. Palmira, whose name I really like. Palmira, what a lovely name! Like herself.

She picked up the file lying on the table and said: "We didn't want to interrupt your sleep, in fact, we should have intervened immediately. But on my instructions, we wanted you to sleep first. When you're tired, we'll start the treatment," she said. She also told me that my arm was broken and had to be put in plaster. That's why I was in so much pain and couldn't move it.

She had already dressed my open wounds that day. **But she told me that she had even more painful news.** I had a fractured skull and needed urgent surgery. They compared it to the tests that had been done when I first came to the hospital, and it wasn't there then. It had obviouslyA been caused by the violence of the bodyguards. "You won't feel anything during the operation. You might be in pain for a few days when you wake up. But we have to treat you first to prevent further damage," she said firmly. I didn't disagree, because Dr. Palmira knew exactly what was right and what was wrong. What she said was what had to be done. Period!

"Before you are taken to the operating room, you will be shown photos by the staff. The policemen are at the door, don't be afraid, we are here for you. **They are here for you, they are here to protect you and put the bad guys and girls where they belong.** You will be confronted soon, we need to take care of this problem first so the investigation can continue without interruption," she said. She must have said it because I was scared. Dr. Palmira was looking after my well-being and her whole team. They stood side by side and made me feel safe. For a long time, maybe for the first time, I experienced such a feeling. They were as safe and warm as a father's house. I would like to thank them.

The policemen were brought into my room and I showed them the ones I could recognize from the photos. After they had identified their addresses, I could tell that what had happened had really happened. I could recognize all the people except for the bodyguards, of which there were seven in total. The bodyguards worked for an agency that identified and located them. The case was immediately brought before a public court. There were also charges of racism. **Those who had kept silent and watched the crime played their part.** While all this was going on, I was undergoing surgery. That was more than three weeks ago, but I still couldn't lift my head. I was very well cared for and surrounded by good people.

Dr. Palmira managed to find Jamelia, the interpreter. She came a few times when I wasn't there. They talked about my children. Her answer was always: I don't know. Then she called the lady from social services and got her name. She didn't have time to come, so she asked them to do it remotely. They had my children. I had no idea how they were or who they were with. **As a mother, I can't explain how painful that is.** It doesn't matter what race you are. Because in motherhood, race doesn't matter. A mother is a mother!

He who does not want to listen to
you will not understand when you shout.
Those who want to understand
you will do it even if you don't talk.

CHAPTER 14

I was here for over a month. I got on very well with Dr. Palmira and her team. They were a balm for my soul. **They took care of my affairs with the immigration office and all the other social services.** Dr. Palmira told me that her brother had just graduated from law school and was now working as a lawyer in her older brother's law firm. They both said they would be happy to help me and take on my case. I gladly agreed. Once I had signed my power of attorney, I no longer had to go to court all the time. It was as if they had agreed to help me too. They helped me a lot and never spared me anything. I thank them all.

Dia, the nurse, went to the refugee shelter to see where my children were, because I was always worried. When she found out that they were no longer there, she called the head doctor, Dr. Palmira, to tell me the news. When I heard this painful news, I lost my mind and started tearing my hair out and crying profusely. I don't know what happened to me, I didn't come to myself for a long time. For almost months.

Dr. Palmira kept telling me that when you lose yourself, you have to accept that you have lost your children too. I memorized this sentence and she helped me to get back on my feet. **Day by day I fought harder, I got up, and day by day I climbed higher and higher.** I never stopped looking for my children. The bomb explosions, the torn people, the soldiers who would eat human flesh were joined by my children in my nightmares. There was no end to these nightmares. I was determined to find my children.

In my later years, I got to know some very optimistic people. Besides Sister Jenny, there were many other optimistic sisters. Silke, Thomas, Andrea, Lena, Monika... I could list many more. Dr. Palmira knew that very well. If I had been discharged in this condition or sent to a refugee home, that would have been the end of me.

"**You're here until you feel better, beautiful woman,**" she said to me.

Dr. Palmira asked me one day during the treatment what my plans were. I replied: "To find my children and keep them with me and to go to the German parliament to account for the use of German-made weapons in the Syrian war". My family was killed with German weapons. The doctor tried to explain this to me in a friendly way.

"The weapons could have been produced in Germany. They could have been bought in Germany. You have to consider that for business reasons. But a German gun can't kill your family by itself. This is a brutal person who did this and he should be held accountable."

She was right in her own way, and what she said made sense to me. But the 12 German trucks were filled to the brim with weapons essential to the war effort, small arms, rifles and bombs. *Should they have been sent into the middle of the war?* I wouldn't have believed it if I hadn't seen it with my own eyes. I saw it with my own eyes. And the American soldiers and tanks protected them and brought them forward. **Isn't that incredible?** *Did they come to bring democracy? Is that how they bring democracy? Like they did in Afghanistan, Pakistan, Iran, Iraq, and Palestine? Is that their understanding of democracy?*

Was their aim to incite their people against their own people, to portray it as a civil war, and to massacre the people by the soldiers they sent? I am young and know nothing about politics. I only think and say what I have seen.

"And will you feel relieved when you go to the Bundestag?" asked Dr. Palmira. "Yes, don't you think they should see and hear the results of their weapons production on a living example?" I asked.

"No, no, I am by no means angry with the German people. On the contrary, I can't thank them enough. They have taken in so many exiles from their country, opened their borders, and given them a roof over their heads. *How could I be angry?* I have made such wonderful friendships, full of love, respect, and compassion. I don't want you to think that way, and I don't want you to think that way either. Because there is no such problem. I have set myself a goal: I want to achieve my goal, with or without beauty, and continue my life with my children in Türkiye."

When I said that, Dr. Palmira seemed to think a little.

She said she had to make a few phone calls, left the room and would explain it to me later. I would wait, that was fine with me as long as there was still hope. Before a few days had passed, Dr. Palmira told me that she was mumbling through her mouth. She told me that her husband's sister was in politics and that if not in parliament, she would put me in a party where I could speak my mind. Since this party was interested in refugee protection laws, it couldn't hurt to voice my problems. Her lawyer brothers also enquired about the whereabouts of my children. They had me sign another power of attorney. They promised me that they would not leave my children alone. **That was good news.** I had the feeling that it was over, but none of it had materialized. Now the real battle for my children began.

Sometimes it's not our body that gets tired,
it's our soul.

CHAPTER 15

The months went by and I turned 22. At least that's what I thought. If the data had been recorded correctly back then, I would have been sure. I felt forty-eight, fifty years old. I was completely exhausted! **I didn't hear anything good from my children, on the contrary, it was as if they had vanished into thin air.** The so-called benevolent lady from the family and social services, who seemed optimistic, had given my children up for adoption to German families. Which families got them is still being investigated. *Who knows what condition they were in, my brave little ones, my children. How could they make such a decision without my permission? Just because their mother was in the hospital? Are the children of every mother who is in a hospital given up for adoption? What kind of decision is that? How can a mother endure such a decision?* They are my source of life. They are my sons, my everything. My wealth, my possessions, my treasure, my resistance. *Why was I standing there without them?*

I was told again and again that I should persevere, that we were almost there. *But how can a mother stand it? What kind of mother can stand it? Who were they given to? where are they? did they want to be given? did I want to give them away?* This pain was a guest in an open place in my womb, infinite. It came like a cheeky guest and settled at my hearth. Only a mother could feel something like that. My heart was on fire and I could hardly take in the therapy sessions I was attending. It was as if I was going in and out.

My intestines were full of pain as if they were overflowing and swelling. Dr. Palmira told me that they didn't want to discharge me from the hospital during this time. Because my recovery wouldn't start until I got through this phase. She said that I would have to deal with my old wounds day by day during this process. And in her way, she was right. **She felt that I would not be able to bear the pain of my children on top of my old wounds.** When I was reunited with my children, I would struggle with my old wounds day after day. To be able to bear all this, I had to face the wounds of my past. My sessions were ineffective because the days went by without me realizing it. The worst thing was that the German Office for Family and Social Affairs had told the court that they had never heard of such a case and that there were no children with these names in their files. The police had searched all the files but found nothing.

I learned that the 150 refugees who had been accommodated in my refugee shelter had been distributed to other refugee shelters throughout Germany. Thanks to my lawyers, the investigation continued at full speed. They eventually found the woman who was working there and reported her to the police. "I don't know, I don't know her," she kept saying. I told her that she had been at the hospital when I was first there, and since she had been on duty, her name must have come up. They were the only visitors apart from you. To find her, you'll have to go through the visitor lists from a few years ago,"

I said. The search began and eventually, her name was found. She could no longer escape me. I was going to keep trying until she gave me my children. We were in the hands of child traffickers. **The woman's apartment was searched and when she was found, she was arrested.** I was one step closer to my children. I couldn't think about my sessions at all. I was on the verge of losing my mind, who knows what happened to them? They were real child traffickers, I had to find my children as soon as possible.

During the interrogation, the policewoman gave several addresses. It was not clear to which families they had handed over the children as they had no names or information. The lawyer was surprised. They explained that it was the first time they had dealt with such a case. It was terrifying. Yes, it was. Even the court staff nodded at this case. It had been changed from a closed to an open trial. **Every courtroom was swarming with journalists.** Now I no longer need to go to the Bundestag and ask my questions. The journalists had already come in droves beforehand. **They even came from local German television to report.** They asked me questions and interviewed me. I was able to express all the pain that had become a wound inside me. **But I didn't see this news on any channel. Although it was said that it would be broadcast on that channel at that time, it was not.**

The lawyers also asked about it, but they said it had not been published. Of course, they can't put such realistic words on the screens and in the newspapers. They don't publish news that opens the eyes of German society. They can only distract them with the fake news they spread every day. *If that's the case, I can think of another example.* Since I came to Germany from Türkiye, I have never seen a German channel broadcasting real news. I'm from Syria, in the middle of a war! Who can bring a real news report that knows the truth, of course! I was wondering who all these channels are working for if they are fed with fake news every day. **There is no place for terror in Islam!** There is no place for terrorism in any religion. It is not necessary to say much on this subject, but I would like to emphasize once again that terrorism has no place anywhere.

Lose...

When you lose something in life that meant a lot to you, it's like losing a piece of yourself.

CHAPTER 16

A few weeks had passed when Dr. Palmira woke me up in a hurry early in the morning. She told me to get dressed quickly, and I hurriedly got dressed and we left the hospital. When I asked her what had happened, she kept saying: "I'll tell you on the way". After we left in her car, I continued to ask her what had happened. **The addresses where my children were staying had been found out.** The police were going to raid them. The lawyer's sister and brother were already on their way. He told me that the police didn't know I was going to be there and that we should be careful. But when she said she didn't want to deprive me of this moment, she was in tears.

When we arrived at the designated address, she calmly parked the car and gave me strict instructions not to get out of the car. She asked me to promise, and I said I would promise, but if my child was in front of me, I didn't know if I could keep it because I was so excited. I would do my best, my excitement was great. After waiting in the car for a while, the police arrived. The doorbell rang and a woman opened the door. It was obvious that it was a rich neighborhood. In Syria, our women look older than they are because they've grown up in a different environment, but in Germany, it wasn't like that.

Before we knew it, the police suddenly pushed the woman against the wall, handcuffed her and put her in the police car. We looked on in bewilderment, not a child in sight. "No, no, I'm taking you to the hospital, you can't watch this,"

Dr. Palmira said to me. The whole time she was trying to calm me down. **When they searched the apartment, they didn't find my child.** What they found was someone else's kidnapped child. It was a terrible child network. Who knows how many other children passed through their hands. When we got to the hospital, they gave me a sedative and I fell asleep. When I woke up again, the decision was unanimous. They told me that they would only inform me about the further course of events when they had found evidence.

If so many children had fallen into their hands, why was this incident never shown on screen? These and similar questions kept running through my mind. I was helpless, the best lawyers were on my side. **Even the judge nodded in agreement.** In this situation, I realized that I was on the right track. Instead of destroying myself even more, I realized that I had to listen to my doctors' advice. If I could get better, I could be a better and stronger mother to my children. **I had to prepare myself for the moment when I would be reunited with my children.** Of course, they would be found today and tomorrow. I was helpless and in pain like I was in the middle of a war. I didn't know how I could get better in this state, but I would try.

The worst pain is the one you can't explain
or show to anyone.

CHAPTER 17

About two months had passed. Following a tip-off, two children were located. **As the children had to be identified, I was called to the police station to check, as a mother, whether they were my children.** Excited, I set off as quickly as possible. Sister Jenny and I went together. The police station was about two and a half hours away. **My heart was pounding like it was about to stop and prayers were coming from my heart the whole way.** When we finally arrived at the police station, we were first subjected to a background check. The children they found were not at the police station. They were kept in a safe place. I was shown their photos and when I saw them, I started kissing and smelling the picture of my children. I screamed and burst into tears, which was the most authentic testimony for the police chief. **Of course, I didn't become that way to make them feel that way.** When I saw my sons, I lost my self-control and acted like any mother. I couldn't help but lose myself in that moment.

I waited a few hours, then I saw my children coming towards me at the beginning of the corridor and I ran towards them. Even though I stumbled and fell, it didn't bother me anymore. I wanted to hug them as quickly as possible. **As I hugged my two babies, I still felt a pang.** One had disappeared.

Mohamed and Ali had been found. **My Omar was still gone.** I was sure we would find him too. I thought *I had my children now,* but the policeman said they would hand them over to the Office for Family and Social Affairs because I didn't have my own apartment and was still in the hospital. "No! No!" I screamed at the top of my lungs, "They've already taken my children away from me. *Why should I give them to them again? Why should I?* I want my children back," I continued to scream. They told me to calm down, I tried to calm down, but *how could I?* They said that if I had my own household, they would give me my children immediately. The court would decide that, not us.

We drove back to the hospital in pain. Of course, they were right. *Did I want to take my children to a psychiatric hospital?* First, of course, I had to be discharged. We talked to Dr. Palmira and the other doctors. One of the doctors said that her children had a house and we could move into the house where her son lived. In the meantime, her children would live on the top floor of her parents' house. She discussed this with her son and he agreed. He told his family, who lived upstairs, that we could move in.

They all tried to sort everything out as quickly as possible. They were all in agreement and did their best to speed things up.

A few days later, I was told that I would soon be discharged. The lady who worked in social services at the hospital told me that I could move in as soon as my household applications and treatments were ready. **They had made sure I had an income, right through to applying for state benefits.**

Once all the procedures were completed, I was able to move into the apartment. In the meantime, my lawyers were not idle. They did everything they could to reunite me with my three sons. I owe them all a great debt of gratitude. *How can I repay them?*

I was released, living in my own apartment for the first time. I can't say enough. **They even enrolled me in a German course.** Dr. Enders' family, whose house I moved into, was a very helpful family. They took me in like their own child. They asked about my daily needs and looked after me. They took me to school and back home again. They took such an interest in me that I could hardly believe it. They were a very sincere family. Of course, they also took pity on me. They had two sons and a daughter. **Not just one, but all of them were such good people!** I am very grateful to all of them.

We will have a court hearing in the next few days. Even before I could see my sons again, they had enrolled them in language courses and schools and taken care of them. My goal was to return to Türkiye. **Even if I didn't want to stay in Germany permanently, I had to abide by the laws and rules.** My sons were of school age and had to continue their education by law so as not to violate compulsory education. **Education was also a priority.** So we had to get by until I found my Omar, who introduced me to my sons every two weeks.

We kissed and smelled each other, but we didn't have a chance to talk and time flew by. But that didn't matter! Even for that short time, I was ready. As long as I could see my sons.

We finally found out about my sons. **My sons were awarded to me by court order.** The world was mine. The only one missing was Omar, but they never stopped looking for him. He was the youngest, he must have been about five years old. *My Omar, my dear son. What if he doesn't remember me? it's been almost three years. Maybe he got used to life in the family he was given to.* I was afraid of that, very afraid. Soon came the good news, they had found my Omar. But it was unbelievable and what I had feared had happened to me. He didn't want me, I didn't doubt the family at the time. But they had nothing to do with it. They said they had adopted him.

"He was given to us because he had no family, he lost his whole family in the war. That's why we took care of him lovingly and sincerely. **We tried to bring him up like our own child,**" they said.

When Omar suddenly saw me, his real mother in front of him, he asked me in German: "**I have a mother, who are you?** And it sounded as if he wanted to shout at me. *What should I do in a situation like this?* The adoptive family had never found me unattractive, they seemed to accept me even though I was veiled. The woman who mothered my Omar was a teacher, and her husband was a mechanical engineer. My son accepted his adoptive family and began to look at me dismissively. **He expressed that he did not accept and reject that I was his mother.** A fire broke out in that corner of my heart that was fanned and could not be put out. I was burning inside.

Germany didn't just take my family away from me with its weapons. They also took my son. After a few years, Omar could no longer speak his mother tongue. He only spoke English and German. He wouldn't even know that there was his mother, whose heart was burning, or that there were his brothers Mohammed and Ali. *What should I do?* Staying is one thing, leaving is another. I was helpless, and I even found it difficult to give the new family my contact details. I was stunned by the situation. My own child didn't want to come back to me. It was as if I could feel it. I thought *something like this would happen to me.* And my fear had come true. It's the mother's heart, she feels it.

We began to discuss the situation in a way that my sons could understand. Together we decided not to disturb their peace. My sons were very wise and mature for their age. They were children who had experienced the war. It was impossible for them not to be mature. We were not undecided whether we should stay or go. We had asked the new family for permission to see my son Omar and to say goodbye to him before we left.

They permitted us to see him, and as a mother on fire, I had to say goodbye to my son. Although he knew we were coming, he hid behind his new mother, whom he had accepted, hugging her tightly and clinging to her leg. When he saw us, it was very difficult to behave like this. After all, it was a mother's heart.

His new mother had gone to a lot of trouble for this situation.

"**Look, my son, this is your family. She is your mother and the others are your brothers.** Please don't be like that. They have come to see you. Look, we will travel to Türkiye to see them. We will stay in touch.

She tried to convince him with a moderate approach. We drank our coffee, they were very hospitable and the lady was a nice person. My son Omar started to make friends with us. He talked and played with his brothers. That made me very happy. I felt a bit reassured. We agreed to stay in touch. I couldn't give my own number yet as I didn't want to stay in Germany forever. I thought *we would be leaving today or tomorrow.* The lady gave me all her information, from the address to the phone numbers. She also said that we could call her whenever we wanted. "You're a mom, I understand that very well, you can talk to him whenever you want," she said.

As they had carried out the adoption legally, the police investigated the adoption of my son Omar. The court ruled that they had done everything legally and there were no problems. When the court ruled that way, our necks were in a noose. My son was illegally taken away from me, but he was legally adopted by a very good family. **His family even tried to support us.** We talked about how well she would take care of my son, and that she would not spare me. When I got up, she asked me if I wanted anything. *As a mother with a burning heart, what could I want?* I just wanted my son to be peaceful and happy and for him not to forget us.

They promised that they would bring him back every year and bring us back together. I was full of hope, even that sentence gave me so much hope as a mother! Of course, I would have preferred to have him with me, but I knew I had to be more sensitive about it because I could see he was in good hands. When I left, it was like a piece of me was ripped out. I left without turning around, but I felt a pain like my insides were being ripped out.

Don't treat people as badly as they are,
treat them as good as you are.

CHAPTER 18

My doctor, my host families at the time, Sister Jenny, Sister Dia, Dr. Palmira, Dr. Enders, Dr. Walter, Sister Magda, Nurse Rainer, and others wholeheartedly supported our return to the Republic of Türkiye. They all agreed to take us under their wing. **What beautiful people there were around me, more than I had ever seen before.** I would be lying if I said I didn't struggle with the feeling that we shouldn't go after making so many friends. But our decision was our choice, and we had decided from the beginning not to stay here forever. I had my reasons for coming here, I dealt with them, and then it was time to go.

The racists who attacked and seriously injured me have been convicted and arrested. They were also sentenced to a fine. So I received a lump sum. That would help us to return. When we got a lump sum, of course, I thought I should report it to the state. I reported that you don't have to help us with money, I had a lump sum. I don't want anything I'm not entitled to.

I was called to the hospital, where the social welfare officer told me that we couldn't leave Germany. He had tried very hard but to no avail. "That's because you don't have passports," he said, asking us why and why not. He went to the immigration authorities on our behalf, but they said there was nothing they could do. We had to apply for a passport at the Syrian consulate. **During the war, the consulate wouldn't issue us passports.** Especially because we had left the country, they didn't recognize such a right. I had to try, I absolutely had to pursue this case. Dr. Palmira's lawyer brothers were back. I had hoped that it might be possible with their help, but I kept getting rejections. Again and again, I was told: "Try again".

We were in Germany for so long that we made good friends who were all very warm and very close to us. **This love became a family friendship. They all had a special place in my heart. They were like a haven I could escape to after the war.** They tried like a mother to heal my wounds. As a result of all these efforts, the consulate finally agreed to issue us a passport in 2017. I have no idea why they did this, but it meant nothing that we got the passport. We had to submit it to immigration and have it processed until we had a passport and a residence permit. When we mentioned our final return, they didn't permit us to leave Germany. That took 3-4 weeks, but that was normal. I used this time to have a nice and healthy time with my good friends. Two of my sons were with me and one with his new family. **We also spent a lot of time with my son Omar. Just as he was getting used to us, the departure came closer and closer.** I was constantly worried that we would hit another obstacle.

Then, the time had come, the immigration office had sent us an email informing us of the appointment. After we had completed the formalities at the immigration office, I wanted to give my son Omar one last hug before we left. Thanks to his new mother, he agreed, and when I realized that she was a very good person, I felt increasingly relieved. Although I was leaving him behind, I no longer had as many doubts as before. **I wanted to entrust my son with the birds of paradise of my childhood and leave Germany.**

A shed with a smile in it is better than a palace crying in it.

CHAPTER 19

Dr. Palmira called me and said I had a visitor. My close friend had come to see me. She said we had met in the refugee center and you know her name, Nurgül Sönmez. When she spoke to me in the nurses' room on the floor where I was hospitalized, my friends who had heard her came and told me. She also left her phone number. She said she wanted to meet me. Yes, I remember this woman, she was Turkish. She was full of compassion, I've never forgotten her face. She must have come to the hospital out of concern. **I was very happy about that because I had thought about it a lot because she had promised to come when I was in hospital for the first time.** I thought *she had kept her promise.*

I immediately called Sister Dia and asked her to translate for me, and she thought it was important and rushed over. We had called at an inconvenient time, but she dropped everything and spoke to me. **The reason she came to the hospital was that she was very worried about me, she called me a lot and she couldn't get me out of her mind since that day.** She often came to the hospital as a visitor when I was still in the locked ward. They said they weren't allowed in and sent her away, but of course, they didn't tell me. I don't even want to remember that floor of the hospital, it was a disaster...

She was very curious about my life and my story. When I asked her why, she said she was a writer. She told me that she had made stories from real life her subject and written them down. She saw me in the refugee home and realized that

I was full of pain. So she said **she wanted to write my story down** and asked me: "Do you want to work on it with me?"

She wanted to write a novel about my life and my experiences. *Was I a heroine? What was I?* I was just a person who had seen and lived through the abyss of suffering. *How could I be the main character?* I looked into the room with a sad smile and cried. But here's what I learned: **Suddenly, a person comes into your life who brings you back to life every time you speak.** And then you realize that you are the protagonist of your life. This woman, this Turkish writer, showed me the treatment I didn't get in the hospital. She taught me how to speak. **With every word that came out of my mouth, she gave me my life back.** The life I thought I didn't have. I had been to so many therapy sessions, but that was nothing compared to her. This woman made me the heroine of my own life.

Now everything was ready, we had packed our bags. Two more days, then it was back to Türkiye. Before we got on the plane, she came in a hurry. **She gave me a tape recorder and blank cassettes. Of course, she also gave me her phone number. She said we would keep in touch and asked us to contact her after we arrived in Türkiye. Then** we talked about the program and how we would work together over this distance. I was very happy. **Even though I had a life story that made me cry, I was happy when I thought about my current situation.** It was really interesting! Some people come into your life and rip your insides out, they make you, not yourself anymore. On the other hand, some people fix you with a single word and help you put your pieces back together. As such people slowly enter my life, I wish for you to have them in your life.

She told me to tell my life story on the tapes as I wanted, to take care of them, and to return them en masse. So we agreed and said goodbye to each other with sadness.

I lost my home, but not my voice.
With every step on foreign ground,
my hope for a new tomorrow grows.

CHAPTER 20

We had finally entered the Republic of Türkiye. But we had no roof over our heads, no work, and no school to go to. I learned a little Turkish in the refugee camp. Over time, I would learn more and master the Turkish language perfectly. It was a great advantage that my sons were still young. They were able to learn and understand Turkish straight away. They were already very intelligent and loved reading.

When we got off the plane, we looked for an apartment to rent, not near the airport, but a little further away. Thanks to them, the Turks were very helpful and no matter who we asked, they did not refuse their support and help. Everyone helped us in a different area. **On the same day, we found a rented apartment, bought our daily food and drink requirements, and settled in.** On one side we ate our food, on the other we poured out what we had in mind. Since we knew that rest and relaxation didn't fill our bellies, we immediately took action.

When I met the landlord at the door, I told him that we were actually looking for a rental apartment where we could stay permanently. **As his wife was there, they welcomed us.** After I offered them drinks in the guest room, we got talking. They told me that they could rent out the house. Luck was on our side. I was very happy. I told them that I would work as soon as I found a job and that they shouldn't worry. **When I told them I didn't know where to enroll my kids in**

school, she said, "Don't worry about it. We'll take care of everything. First, you have to tell the municipality that you live here and register yourself and your children". Of course, I did that and there was also someone who helped me with it. You can't contradict the state, you can't fight the state. If I wanted to stay and live in the Republic of Türkiye, I had to abide by the laws and regulations. I tried to fulfill everything that had to be fulfilled.

I had completed the residence procedure and was sent to the Ministry of National Education to enroll my sons in school. Our situation didn't allow us to wait, so I immediately started looking for work. I would take any job, no matter what. All of our new neighbors were closer to us than blood relatives. **Everyone tried to help us.** I can't thank them enough. They are all so warm and friendly! There was always a smile on their faces. Of course, they didn't just walk around smiling, but they never withheld their smiles from us.

Thanks to good people, we started our new life full of strength and happiness. As I lay in bed with my sons, we began to talk. I felt so refreshed as if I was experiencing this feeling for the first time. **The more I talked, the more relieved I became.** This pain, this heavy burden had fallen from my shoulders. **This pain on my shoulders taught me how important it is to speak.**

Speaking has taught me a lot. My back, which I used to have to walk with four bends, became straighter day by day. Day by day, I began to walk upright. I had done nothing wrong, so I began to think, *why should I bow my head? I haven't done anything to anyone,* so this discomfort is like a heavy burden on my shoulders!

I opened the tapes and started to record my speeches. **The speech recordings helped me more than the therapy sessions at the hospital.** I was now a breadwinner. I could protect and care for my children.

By the way, after my life had calmed down again, I gave Mrs. Nurgül my contact details. I told her that I had started recording. She was very happy about it. "**Relax, don't neglect your new routine!**" she said. "No, no!" I said hastily, interrupting her. "If you hadn't told me to talk, I might not have been able to open up to so many people today. Maybe I wouldn't have been able to build a new routine so quickly today. **The Turkish people around me accepted me and took me into their midst.** When my sons were out and about, my neighbors looked after them, even if I didn't.

Every evening, after I had put my sons to bed, I picked up the tape recorder and told them what was going on inside me, without a dot or a comma, until I fell asleep. **My pain, my sadness, myself... I told you everything.**

Now I was at the end of my story and my speech. I told everything from beginning to end. Mrs. Nurgül had come to Ankara. At the end of a day in which we had talked a lot, she had left and taken the tapes with her.

Mrs. Nurgül told me that from the moment I left the refugee camp in Türkiye and traveled to Germany, 1001/ thousand and one day had passed until my return. Yes, she was right. I didn't count the days, but I think it must have been that many. How right she was. As oriental as that may sound, in reality, it's not.

Instead of 1001 nights - a thousand and one days!

Nurgül Sönmez

– Schriftstellerin –

A child who survived the war,
knows the value of school,
reading, books and education.

THE END

Matilda Türkçe

Savaşın İçinden Bir Kelebek

Sert Kapak - İnce Kapak - e-kitap

Matilda Deutsch

Ein Schmetterling inmitten des Krieges

Paperback - Hardcover - e-book

Matilda English

A butterfly through the war

Paperback - Hardcover - e-book

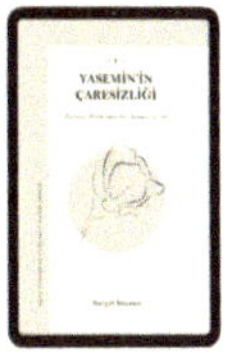

Yasemin'in Çaresizliği - 1 Türkçe

Binlerce Yasemin'den Bir Yasemin'in Sesi

Sert Kapak - İnce Kapak - e-kitap

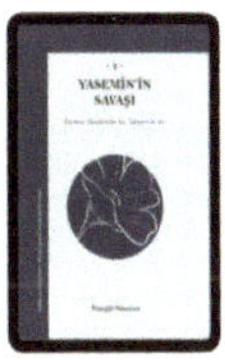

Yasemin'in Savaşı - 2 Türkçe

Binlerce Yasemin'den Bir Yasemin'in Sesi

Sert Kapak - İnce Kapak - e-kitap

Yasemin'in İntikamı - 3 Türkçe

Binlerce Yasemin'den Bir Yasemin'in Sesi

Sert Kapak - İnce Kapak - e-kitap

Yasemins Verzweiflung - 1 Deutsch

Eine Stimme unter Tausenden

Paperback - Hardcover - e-book

Yasemins Kampf - 2 Deutsch

Eine Stimme unter Tausenden

Paperback - Hardcover - e-book

Yasemins Rache - 3 Deutsch

Eine Stimme unter Tausenden

Paperback - Hardcover - e-book

Yasemins Desperation - 1 English

One voice among thousands

Paperback - Hardcover - e-book

Yasemins Struggle - 2 English

One voice among thousands

Paperback - Hardcover - e-book

Yasemins Revenge - 3 English

One voice among thousands

Paperback - Hardcover - e-book

1001 Gece Yerine Bin Bir Gün Türkçe

"Özgürlüğe süzülen bir mülteci"

Sert Kapak - İnce Kapak - e-kitap

Statt 1001 Nacht - Tausendundein Tag Deutsch

"Weg in die Freiheit"

Paperback - Hardcover - e-book

Instead Of 1001 Night – One Thousand and One Day English

"A refugee soaring to freedom"

Paperback - Hardcover - e-book

Maarouf Türkçe

"Vatanı tarafından terk edilmiş bir adamın, inanılmaz öyküsü"

Sert Kapak - İnce Kapak - e-kitap

Maarouf Deutsch

"Ein Mann, der von seiner Heimat verlassen wurde"

Paperback - Hardcover - e-book

Maarouf English

"The incredible story of a man abandoned his homeland by force"

Paperback - Hardcover - e-book

■ **Wir bieten:**

In den Sprachen Deutsch, Englisch, Türkisch und Französisch fachgerechte literarische Buchübersetzung an. Zusätzlich;

- Lektorat - Deutsch, Englisch, Türkisch, Französisch
- Korrekturlesen - Deutsch, Englisch, Türkisch, Französisch

Sie haben auch Interesse Ihr Werk oder Ihre Werke literarisch zu Übersetzen und von unseren zusätzlichen Dienstleistungen zu profitieren (Lektorat, Korrekturlesen, Buchcover Design, Illustration & Buchsatz).

Dann schicken Sie uns Ihre Anfrage per Email.

■ **We offer:**

Professional literary book translation in German, English, Turkish and French.

- Editing - German, English, Turkish, French
- Droofreading - German, English, Turkish, French

You are also interested in literary translation of your work(s) and benefit from our additional services (Editing, droofreading, book cover design, illustration & book typesetting).

Then send us your request by email.